Frolick

Jennifer Green-Neff

FROLICK © 2025, Jennifer Green-Neff

ISBN (Paperback): 979-8-9928037-4-7
ISBN (eBook): 979-8-9928037-5-4
ISBN (Hardcover): 979-8-9928037-9-2

Published by Jennifer Green-Neff
Frolickbook.com

Cover design by Paura Marrero
Interior design by Jennifer Green-Neff
Editing by Amber Elizabeth and Samantha Lane

Printed in the United States of America.
First Edition: 2025

For permissions, inquiries, or bulk purchases,
contact: info@frolickbook.com

Dedication Page

For the ones who never settled. For those who learned, laughed through heartbreak, and turned their scars into stories worth telling. And for anyone who's ever frolicked their way through love, chaos, and self-discovery. This one's for you.

Literary Note

Yes, I'm aware that Frolick isn't the traditional spelling, but Sam's life isn't traditional. Consider this my grammatically rebellious streak.

Sam: The Brains

"Truth Hurts – Lizzo"

This is the story of a girl who set her world on fire and somehow survived the aftermath.

And that girl? It's me. Sam. Well, Samantha if I'm in trouble.

I'm 5'9", lanky, and didn't fully come into my own until my senior year of high school—and even then, it was questionable. My limbs felt too long for my body, like a baby giraffe taking its first steps, except I had to do it in front of an audience of ruthless teenagers.

I spent most of my adolescence towering over the girls and boys, which meant I never quite fit into either group. To make matters worse, I grew up switching schools every two years.

My father was a Navy SEAL, which meant our zip code was about as permanent as a spray tan in a rainstorm. Every couple of years we packed up our lives and started over somewhere new. New school. New hallways. New lunch tables already claimed by territorial cliques.

Spoiler Alert: I've been bullied, spit on, and thrown into lockers.

Middle school was like the *Hunger Games,* but with acne and mean girls. It was a goddamn war zone. Nothing breeds cruelty quite like preteens with raging hormones and unchecked insecurities.

And dating, forget it. I was as inexperienced as they come. I hadn't so much as kissed a boy until my senior year of high school and that was a dumpster fire.

Well, okay, that's not entirely accurate. Technically, I had my *first* first kiss in third grade.

The coolest boy in class—"coolest" meaning he had a gelled-up faux hawk and could burp the alphabet—walked up to me at recess, kissed me full on the mouth, and then tried to slip me tongue.

At eight years old.

I remember standing there, completely stunned, feeling his weird, slimy little tongue poking at my lips like a feral cat trying to escape a bathtub. It was horrifying. I think I blacked out for a second.

Needless to say, my "actual" first kiss in high school happened in a very similar fashion. I was stunned and grossed out. Apparently, some things never change.

This is my story. Me in a nutshell. It's messy and ugly, but also poetic and beautiful.

Enjoy. Or don't. That's entirely up to you.

I remember bits and pieces from my childhood. Some memories are so vivid, it's like they just happened yesterday. Others, not so much.

I recall my parents being very strict. Both of them. My mom was both the matriarch and the patriarch, the kind of woman who could send a house into DEFCON 1 with a single side-eye. I walked on eggshells around her, but she was also a constant force who shaped me into the independent woman I am today. My dad was gone a lot—sometimes for work, top-secret missions overseas we weren't allowed to ask about, and sometimes for hunting season. And if that happened to fall on my birthday, well, tough luck for me.

Then there was my sister. We weren't the type to braid each other's hair or whisper secrets under the covers. She steered clear of me like I had a contagious disease, which meant when I needed help navigating the mysteries of being a girl—how to straighten my hair, put in a tampon, or, you know, what masturbation meant—I was on my own. But despite pretending I didn't exist 99% of the time, she was fiercely protective. She may have barely tolerated me, but if someone else dared to make fun of me, she would eviscerate them on the spot. And that was love.

I needed my family. They were the only constant in my life. The only people who had been there through every move, every awkward first day, every stupid nickname I got saddled with in a new school.

I don't remember being overly sad or traumatized in my child-hood. A kid who's bullied would feel that, right? I also didn't have many friends, and I don't remember caring much. There was no void to fill, no deep longing for companionship. That's the im-portance of the close-knit relationship I had with my family. They were my safe space. My reprieve from assholes. My everything.

Besides, I wasn't lonely. I had an overactive imagination and would entertain myself for hours. I could turn an empty room into a full-fledged telenovela. I'd create elaborate stories, giving my dolls scandalous backstories and dramatic love triangles long before I even understood what romance was. I was completely content in my little world.

~ell~

Maybe it was the years of bullying that hardened me to experienc-ing actual fear because there were only a few things in this world that truly terrified me.

Chainsaws. Obviously. Clowns. Who isn't? Centipedes. They will forever haunt my dreams.

And lastly – **Boys.**

Unlike chainsaws, clowns, and centipedes, boys were a different kind of terrifying. A kind that followed me around. A kind that lived in my own head, no chainsaw-wielding maniac required.

The terror stemmed from one fundamental truth: I was painfully, catastrophically inexperienced.

First, there was the kissing crisis. For years, I obsessed over the fact that I had never kissed anyone. What if I was bad at it? What if my lips just sat there like two lifeless slugs? What if my teeth got in the way? What if I accidentally exhaled so hard into their mouth that I inflated them like a balloon animal? These were real concerns.

Then, miraculously, I broke the seal. I had my first real kiss. And while it wasn't exactly a scene from a romance novel, it was fine. Nothing exploded and no one died.

Technically, I survived.

But, my idiot brain decided to upgrade my fears. Because once I kissed someone, I suddenly had to start worrying about everything that came after kissing. Which, let's be honest, was so much worse.

Like, you want to put what, where?! And you genuinely think that's going to fit?! Are you sure?! Because, logistically speaking, that does not seem correct.

And don't even get me started on the mechanics. The pressure of knowing what to do. The fear of making a terrible first impression. The absolute horror of not knowing where to put my hands. Was I supposed to breathe? Hold my breath? Blink? Make eye contact? Was there a correct facial expression for this?!

I had no idea. And that was terrifying.

Let's face it, clowns might chase you. Chainsaws might decapitate you. Centipedes might hide in your dresser drawers. *IYKYK.*

But boys could ruin you and that was a whole different level of scary.

—◦◦◦—

I've learned a lot over the years.

For starters, Spam and rice should be their own food group. Next, I know how to spot a bad kisser—if they lead with tongue, abort mission. And I've learned how to tell when someone's about to break your heart. Spoiler: if they're a surfer, run.

But the most important lesson is that people will hurt you. Sometimes on purpose, sometimes by accident, and sometimes because they're just emotionally stunted gremlins masquerading as functioning adults.

And you can either let them burn you, again and again, or you can light the damn match yourself.

And I did just that. Frolicked about, and set a few things ablaze along the way.

Craig: The First Taste

"First Date – Blink 182"

My first real college boyfriend broke things off with a text message.

Not a dramatic breakup. Not a long emotional speech.

Just this:

Craig: *Hey, I think we should cool it for a while. I'm kinda in demand right now.*

I stared at my phone. Was he serious? I had never laughed so hard in my life. Craig – sweet, inexperienced Craig – was **in demand**?

I did what any female in this situation would do, I sent a screenshot to my BFF group chat.

Me: *I'm screaming. Please tell me this is a joke.*

Georgia: *This man thinks he's on a press tour for his debut album.*

Jenn: *WHO DEMANDED HIM? I need names.*

Me: *I need to see the waiting list.*

Georgia: *Maybe it's a small demand? Like, three people?*

Jenn: *One of them is his mom.*

I was crying laughing. But instead of ignoring him, I decided to play along.

Me: *Oh wow, "in demand"? Are you booked through next semester? Or do I need to speak to your agent?*
Craig: *Haha, very funny.*
Me: *Serious question. Did you rehearse this or did it just come to you?*

Apparently, the girls were lining up to get a piece of him.

I wasn't even upset. If anything, I was impressed by his sudden confidence. So I let it roll off my back and continued teasing him about it.

And it worked, because he was banging down my door, backpedaling and telling me he'd made a mistake, that he'd had a lapse in judgment.

I wasn't mad, but I wasn't about to let him off easy, either.

———ell———

To understand why Craig's sudden "in demand" era was so funny to me, you need to understand one thing about my love life at the time: I had absolutely no idea what I was doing.

I was very inexperienced heading into college. I had a boyfriend right out of high school named Jason. He was a blip in my story, a footnote at best. But if nothing else, Jason taught me how to kiss. And my God, could that man kiss.

We'd make out for hours, tangled up in each other, his hands in my hair, mine gripping his shirt, completely lost in it, listening to Dave Matthews play in the background. But that's where it stopped. I always stopped it. I wasn't ready for more, and Jason was heading out of state for school anyway.

By the time summer ended, I was single and stepping onto campus with barely any experience beyond that of a well-practiced lip lock.

At that age, I didn't know if I had a type. I knew who I thought was good-looking, but due to my inexperience, I couldn't nail down my exact preferences. I think I was more fascinated by the *idea* of liking someone than actually knowing what I wanted. Crushes were more about butterflies than real attraction.

Besides, the idea of going further was terrifying. My main concern was wondering if it would hurt. And I don't care who you are, a female's first time is not a pleasant experience. So instead of facing that fear, I became a serial kisser.

By sophomore year, the boys at the fraternity houses called me the *Kissing Bandit*. I wish I could make that shit up.

I deserved it, though. I had a tendency to hang out with guys, flirt, lead up to the moment, and then after a kiss, I'd be out.

Peace. Gone.

I'd dodge their calls, ignore their texts, and pretend the whole thing never happened. Not because they were terrible (well, sometimes they were), but because I wasn't ready for what might come next.

I never admitted it to anyone, but it was a defense mechanism. The second I kissed them, I cut them at the knees before they could push for more. Poor bastards probably thought it was something they did. And let's be clear, sometimes it was.

This one wore a mank top - a man in a tank top. *Unforgivable.*
This one bathed in cologne that suffocated me.
This one gazed into my eyes too long. Instant ick.

And then there was Craig.

Craig was cute. That was the best way to describe him. Not hot. Not rugged. Just boy-next-door cute.

He wasn't a man's man. He was 5'10 with a boyish face. Lean but muscular build, dark hair, and brown eyes. He looked like someone's first boyfriend. Someone's safe choice.

And maybe that's what I liked about him. I was inexperienced and so was he.

On paper, we had nothing in common except one thing.
The thing I needed most: inexperience.

Our first kiss wasn't the kind that stopped time or made my knees weak. It was fine. But unlike all the others before him, I didn't disappear afterward.

We kissed again. And again. That alone set him apart.

———*ele*———

The night Craig told me he kissed someone else, I didn't react. We weren't exclusive. I had no right to be upset. But still, it stung.

We were sitting in his dorm room, his voice full of regret, his eyes searching mine for some kind of reaction.

"I, uh—" Craig exhaled, rubbing the back of his neck. "I just wanted to be honest with you."

I said nothing.

He shifted uncomfortably. "It didn't mean anything. It was just... it just happened."

Silence.

"I was drunk," he added. "Like, really drunk. I barely even remember it."

I raised an eyebrow.

Craig let out a nervous laugh. "You're freaking me out. Can you say something?"

I blinked, my throat tight, my stomach a sinking pit.

He sighed. "Are you mad?"

Still, I said nothing.

"Are you okay?" he asked.

I swallowed the lump in my throat, forcing a shrug.

Craig's face fell.

"Sam. Please?" He ran a hand over his face, exasperated now.

I just sat there. Silent.

"I'm so sorry. It'll never happen again," Craig kept apologizing. Kept waiting for me to say something.

But I couldn't. I wasn't intentionally being theatrical. I literally couldn't find words. I simply remained silent.

I also didn't cry even though it was my first taste of what it felt like to be betrayed by a boy. And this would be the first of many male betrayals in my life.

I should have walked away then.
But I didn't.

We didn't speak for weeks after Kissgate. I figured that was it. But then one of his fraternity brothers reached out, practically begging me to give Craig another chance.

"He's miserable," he told me. "Moping around the house. It's pathetic."

That should've been a red flag—the level of sensitivity I was about to encounter with this man—but against my better judgment, I gave Craig another shot.

The text I sent started out casual.

Me: *Hey.*
Craig: *Hey back.*

Then nothing. Figured I'd let him suffer and see what hole he'd dig.

Craig: *I messed up.*

Still no response.

Craig: *I miss you.*

Silence. But only because I was blowdrying my hair and didn't see the text come through.

Then he switched to desperation.

Craig: *I haven't been able to sleep.*
Craig: *I had a dream you were at the frat house and I woke up and you weren't there and I almost cried.*
Me: *Did you just admit to almost crying?*
Craig: *I mean... maybe.*
Me: *That's embarrassing for you.*

I thought about leaving it there. I sighed, pinching the bridge of my nose. I should have left him in his self-inflicted misery, but instead, I rolled my eyes and sent one last text.

Me: *Wanna go get some breakfast?*

His response came so fast.

Craig: *ABSOLUTELY!*

I smirked. God, he was predictable.

*　　　✿✿✿*

College was a lot of things—stressful, fun, indulgent, chaotic—but if there was one thing our school took ridiculously seriously, it was Greek Week.

Every year, sororities and fraternities squared off in a series of competitions that ranged from the mildly athletic to the downright absurd.

And this year. Flag football.

A brutal, no-mercy battle between my sorority and Craig's fraternity. Bragging rights were at stake. People trained for this shit. Not me, obviously. But other people.

Craig, on the other hand, was very into it. He'd been talking about it for weeks, hyping up his fraternity's "strategy." As if a group of beer-fueled guys in cargo shorts were suddenly the NFL.

The game was intense. I may have been half-assing it, but some of these cats were out for blood. And right when the game was at peak chaos, I saw Craig running toward the end zone, eyes locked on a pass sailing through the air. This was his moment. His big catch.

And then, he collided with another one of his fraternity brothers.

He still managed to catch the ball. Score!!! But, when they went down in a tangled mess, the fraternity brother's foot made contact with Craig's scrotum. And not a light tap. A full-force, cleat-to-the-crotch, impact.

Craig made a noise that I'm pretty sure wasn't human, collapsed to the ground, and rolled onto his side, clutching his groin like he had just taken a bullet.

"Oh my God," someone whispered. "I think we killed him."

I ran over, torn between laughing and genuinely worrying that his future children had just been permanently erased from existence.

"Babe, are you okay?" I asked, hovering awkwardly as he groaned in pure agony.

He couldn't even speak. Just rolled onto his back, staring at the sky like he was making peace with his life choices.

A few of his fraternity brothers knelt beside him, highly concerned for the fate of his testicles.

"Dude," one of them whispered. "Are they still attached?"

Craig just whimpered.

The game was over. There was no recovering from this. His fraternity forfeited and my sorority celebrated like we had just won the fucking Super Bowl.

But Craig spent the rest of the day in bed, nursing what would later become a truly horrifying bruise. And then, because I should have known better, he texted me.

Craig: *You have to come look at it.*
Me: *Excuse me?*
Craig: *It's bad. Like really bad. I think I need a second opinion.*
Me: *Craig. I love you. But I am NOT looking at your injured nutsack.*
Craig: *Just a quick glance?*
Me: *Absolutely not.*
Craig: *I'd do it for you.*
Me: *No you wouldn't. I don't have balls.*

After several failed attempts to get me to inspect the damage, Craig finally went to the campus nurse, who (according to him) "winced and immediately handed me an ice pack."

But even though I refused to play nurse initially, I did make him a care basket. Ice packs, a ridiculous amount of ibuprofen, and a tub of ice cream labeled "For Your Balls & Your Soul."

Because I might not have been ready to see his scrotum, but I was still a supportive girlfriend.

—ele—

With Craig, it was easy. Easy, because we were both inexperienced. Despite everything, we were each other's first for a lot of things. And that meant something.

Or at least, I convinced myself it did.

The fear I had with other guys—the pressure and the unspoken expectations—faded with Craig. He never made me feel like I had to rush. Never made me feel like I was on some kind of countdown clock.

He put me at ease constantly. With him, there was no urgency or impatience. Just two people figuring things out at their own pace.

Craig wasn't the guy trying to push me too far, too fast. He wasn't the one with a game plan, waiting for the right moment to cash in on whatever he thought he was owed.

We took our time and we learned together.

There were no expectations, no sudden moves, and no fear of disappointing someone or doing something wrong. It was just exploration at our own speed.

And for once, I wasn't afraid of what came next. Instead, I found myself wanting to experience it all with him.

—ele—

Our first time was at a DoubleTree at the oceanfront. Because nothing says romance like a mid-tier hotel with free cookies.

It was the night of our Panhellenic formal. A night where my sorority sisters wore more sparkles than a preteen at a Taylor Swift concert, and the fraternity brothers looked like they were auditioning for a lead role on *Peaky Blinders*.

I remember the buzz of the night—the dancing, the endless plates of subpar chicken and overcooked green beans, the alcohol we weren't supposed to have but somehow always did. And underneath it all, there was this electric undercurrent of anticipation.

We had a room reserved. We knew we wanted to be each other's first. It wasn't spontaneous or fueled by too many drinks. It was a joint decision, a milestone, and something we both wanted to experience together.

From the moment we checked in, the air felt heavier, like the night had a purpose. Because we both knew exactly what was coming next.

By the time we made it back to the room, the reality of it all hit me.

Oh shit.

There were a lot of nerves but there was also an undercurrent of excitement. The sheer absurdity of checking off 'loses virginity' like it was just another item on a to-do list, still makes me laugh to this day.

But, unlike most first-timers, we didn't rush into it.

First, we showered. Separately. Because we were still in the 'nervous and awkward' phase of this adventure. Then, we did what any couple about to embark on a monumental life experience would do—we ate a damn cookie. Because when DoubleTree hands you a warm chocolate chip cookie, you don't say no.

I sat on the bed, nibbling at the edges, stalling, feeling the weight of Craig moving around the room. I wasn't scared, exactly. Just processing.

And then, it happened, we started exploring.

Here's the truth about virgins and their first time: They're not perfect. There are no fireworks or slow-motion movie moments. No perfectly choreographed intimacy or flawless execution. It's hesitant, unsure, and a little clumsy.

We kissed, then we fumbled, but we ultimately figured things out in real time. It was new and weird and exciting all at once. And, if I'm being honest, it was nice.

Not earth-shattering or mind-blowing. But sweet and safe. Ours.

And for a first time, that's all you can really ask for.

We lay there afterward, his arm draped over me, the TV humming in the background. I think *Friends* was on. Something familiar and comforting. I felt lighter, not different or suddenly enlightened, just content.

And then, the frat house showed up.

BANG. BANG. BANG.

Craig and I both shot upright.

From the other side of the door came a chorus of whoops and whistles, laughter, and *Craig, you absolute legend!*

Oh my God.

I stared at him. "How the hell do they know our room number?"

Craig groaned, covering his face with a pillow.

What's it like having those "legs for days" wrapped around you?

For fucks sake.

Craig chuckled, shaking his head. "They're never going to let me live this down."

I grinned, rolling onto my side to face him. "Legs for days, huh?"

He exhaled a laugh, lacing his fingers through mine. And just like that, the world outside didn't matter. It was a nice first time. A nice beginning.

Eventually, Craig and I would become a master class in making love.

But that night, it was just two people, figuring it out together. And that was enough.

—ee—

It was a Thursday night, which meant one thing and one thing only—college students taking over local dive bars like we owned them.

This particular watering hole was exactly what you'd expect. Sticky floors with dim lighting and a jukebox playing the kind of god-awful music that should be illegal but somehow always got the whole bar singing.

We lingered by the dartboard missing more darts than it held, because drunk people and sharp objects were a dangerous combination.

We were rowdy but harmless, taking shots, and singing aggressively off-key to whatever classic rock song some idiot paid money to play on repeat. Half our college was there, packed shoulder to shoulder, the smell of stale beer thick in the air.

At some point, I found myself in a random conversation with a guy from another fraternity. I didn't know him well, but we'd both been assigned the same English Lit project. We were laughing and chatting about how our professor was a sadist for making us analyze 19th-century poetry while hungover.

Normal conversation. Completely innocent. Until it wasn't. Out of nowhere, he tilted his head, smirking, and said,

"So, what do you see in Craig?"

I laughed at first, thinking it was a half-drunk joke, something casual.

But then, he kept going. Right there, with Craig sitting next to me.

"Seriously," the guy continued, eyes flicking toward Craig, then back at me. "You could do so much better."

Craig let out a small laugh, at first playing along, assuming it was just another dumb fraternity joke.

But this guy, he wasn't stopping.

He leaned in, voice dropping an octave, getting bolder with every drink he had in his system.

"I mean, come on. You're way too hot for him."

Silence. And not the good kind. The kind where every nearby conversation pauses like the whole bar could sense the shift in energy.

Craig stiffened next to me. His grip on his beer tightened, his shoulders locked.

I felt a rush of pure, molten fury. Not just for Craig but for anyone who had ever been humiliated for no reason. For anyone who had ever been deemed 'not good enough' in front of a damn audience.

I turned to the guy, fire in my veins, and before I could stop myself, I said—

"You clearly haven't seen the size of his dick."

That did it. The guy blinked. The smirk, gone. The arrogance, shattered.

Craig choked on his drink. A few people nearby started snickering.

I just stared at him and took a sip of my cocktail like I hadn't just verbally eviscerated this man and watched his manhood invert. The guy mumbled something incoherent, probably about needing another beer, and quickly disappeared into the crowd.

Good. Rot in your humiliation.

Craig turned to me, his mouth slightly open. "Did you just?"

"Yes."

He stared for a second, then let out a sharp, surprised laugh. He kissed me hard and grabbed my hand. We just sat there in silence holding hands.

But the energy had changed. The thing was that wasn't the first time I'd heard it. People questioned us a lot. We got the same backhanded comments over and over again.

"You could do better."
"You're too hot for him."
"Why him?"

At first, I brushed it off. It didn't matter what other people thought. But that night, something shifted.

Because the truth—the one I didn't want to say out loud—was that on some level, I had started to believe them.

Maybe I was out of his league. Maybe the thing that initially drew me to him, his inexperience, his patience, his ease, was no longer something I needed. Maybe I had outgrown him.

And I hated myself for even entertaining the thought.

I glanced at Craig, who was still laughing at the absurdity of the moment, still completely unaware of the internal war raging in my head.

And for the first time, I felt the tiniest crack in the foundation of what we had built.

Because when enough people say the same thing over and over again, eventually, you start to wonder if they're right.

—–ell—–

My family, we're a unit. Tight-knit, unshakable. We ride hard for each other.

My mother and sister are my best friends. My father is my hero.

Needless to say, we welcome people in. Like really welcome them in. You come to our house, you leave with a full belly, a to-go plate, and the undeniable feeling that—for at least a little while—you were part of something.

That's just what we do.

So when Craig first met my family, they treated him like he'd always been there. Instantly folded him into our world.

Every Sunday dinner, Craig was at the table, laughing at my dad's bad jokes, winning over my mom without even trying, getting side-eyes from my sister that I knew meant approval. He became a fixture, seamlessly woven into the rhythm of our lives.

So when he invited me to upstate New York that summer to meet his family, I was excited. Confident, even. Because naturally, I assumed it would be the same. I thought warmth was universal. That hospitality was just what people did.

Nope. I was dead wrong.

―――

We pulled up to a modest two-story house—the kind of place that screamed respectable family with deep roots. The air was crisp and intoxicating, filled with the aroma of something delicious baking in the oven.

I stepped out of the car, smoothed my shirt, and reminded myself to be on my best behavior. Smile. Be polite. Win them over.

Spoiler: they were not interested in being won.

His father was nice enough. His mother tolerated me. His sister? Oh, his sister hated my fucking guts. She didn't even try to hide it.

From the moment I walked through the door, I felt it. The cold glances, the clipped responses, the way she barely acknowledged my existence unless it was absolutely necessary. It wasn't outright hostility. No, that would've been easier to deal with. This was worse. This was pure, silent loathing, rolling off her in waves—thick, heavy, and impossible to ignore. It oozed from her like a goddamn fog machine at a haunted house.

Dinner was a disaster. The conversation at the table felt forced and the tension was palpable. Every time I spoke, his sister just stared. Not even subtly—just full-on, deadpan, blinking slow like a serial killer.

I glanced at Craig, silently pleading for help. He just gave me a small, nervous smile and shoveled more pasta into his mouth like it was his only job in life.

His mother asked me a few polite questions. I answered them. His father cracked a joke, and I laughed. His sister, however, she remained quiet.

Well, that's a lie. At one point, I asked her a harmless question about her favorite part of growing up in West Islip. Her response? "Nothing worth mentioning."

Which, on one hand, fair. But on the other hand—like, fuck you very much.

Otherwise, it was silence from her. Pure. Fucking. Silence.

I took another bite of my salad and resisted the urge to ask, "So, what exactly is your problem with me?"

But I refrained out of respect for Craig.

I wish I could say there was some defining moment where she and I just didn't click. But there wasn't. She simply hated me.

And honestly, by the end of the night, I hated her right back.

___ee___

The only good thing about that entire trip was that Craig and I christened every damn room in that house.

Kitchen. Check. His childhood bedroom. Check. Guest room. Double check.

Because, of course, they weren't about to give us a room to share. His parents and sister weren't home most of the time, and when they were, it didn't stop us.

Maybe it was the secrecy or the tension I felt every second I was in that house. Shit, maybe I just needed something—anything—to distract myself from the sinking realization that this wasn't working.

First, it was the constant comments from friends about me being out of his league—that's what planted the seed.

Then came the cold shoulder from his family, the silent rejection that wrapped itself around me like I was back in middle school.

And that's all it took for me to realize that we weren't working anymore.

We'd only been at his family's house for two days, and I already needed a break, so Craig took me to his favorite Italian restaurant for dinner.

Honestly, it was a really nice night. For a minute, it almost felt normal, like the tension back at the house wasn't eating me alive. But the moment we pulled into his parents' driveway, that warm, full feeling in my stomach twisted into something else entirely. Dread.

He put the car in park and turned toward the house. But I didn't move. I wasn't ready to go back inside. I wasn't ready to step back into that hostile, awkward space where his sister glared at me like I personally burned her childhood diary.

I needed an escape. A moment to just not exist in that reality.

So, instead of opening the car door, I turned to Craig, grabbed his face, and kissed him like my life depended on it. Like I was starving, and he was the nourishment I needed. His surprise lasted all of three seconds before he kissed me back, hands immediately gripping my face.

It wasn't sweet or slow. It was messy, desperate, and reckless. I didn't care if someone saw us. I almost wanted them to. Let his sister hate me. Let his mother tolerate me. They already didn't like me, so why not give them a real reason?

We made it inside—barely. By some miracle, the house was quiet. The lights were dim. No sounds from upstairs. It was like the universe had gifted me this one moment of reckless abandon.

I grabbed Craig's hand and pulled him toward the living room. The couch. Too obvious. The floor. Perfect.

We collapsed onto the rug, his hands already under my dress, my fingers tangled in his hair. I barely had time to breathe before his lips were on my neck, his breath hot against my skin, his hands quickly removing my panties. We made love on the carpet, and let the TV drown out any noises.

It was risky and I didn't care. Because at that moment, I wanted to forget. Forget that his family didn't like me. Forget that we weren't working anymore. Forget that, soon, I'd have to face the reality that I didn't love him the way I once thought I did.

But for now, I let myself get lost in him.

By the time the trip was over, I was more than ready to go home. It had only been a week and it felt like an eternity.

Craig, oblivious, held my hand as we packed up the car, kissed my temple before pulling onto the highway, and played his terrible pop-tart playlist like nothing had changed. But something had.

His family made me question everything. And the more I thought about it, the more I realized they weren't the problem.

Because the truth is that I didn't want to be with Craig anymore.

And after this trip, I couldn't ignore it. My decision had been made.

The first time I tried to break up with Craig, there were a lot of tears.

From him, not me.

Craig was a bit of a crier.

And look, I'm not saying there's anything wrong with men show-ing emotions. At the time, it made me uncomfortable. My father, a retired Navy Seal, didn't even cry at his own parents' funeral. So, Craig crying at everything was overwhelming.

He'd bring me flowers, tears in his eyes. He'd write me a sweet poem, tears in his eyes. We'd make love, and you guessed it. Tears. In. His. Eyes.

It was too much. Too much fucking emotion. And I was suffocat-ing.

One night, on our way back from yet another forgettable meal in the cafeteria, something in me just halted. Mid-step, I stopped cold, turned, and without saying a word, sat down on the steps of his dorm building. I couldn't keep walking like everything was fine, because it wasn't.

We were in a stairwell. **A stairwell.**

Of all the places on campus to end a relationship, my dumb ass chose a concrete staircase with bad lighting and zero privacy. I had no idea why. Maybe I thought a public place would lessen the blow. Maybe I thought the fluorescent lights and dirty handrails would make it feel less tragic. Or maybe I just panicked and sat down, and he followed, and before I knew it, I was dumping him next to a vending machine that smelled like Nacho Cheese Doritos.

Not exactly the cinematic breakup moment you see in the movies. But there we were.

"This isn't working," I said, my voice steady, because I had rehearsed this.

Craig blinked at me, his eyes already starting to gloss over. *Oh no. Here we go.*

"What isn't working," he said, knowing the answer already.

"Craig, don't make me say it," I responded, exhausted already.

He just stared at me.

"Us, Craig. Us." I finally admitted.

"I love you," he blurted out, his voice cracking. "I don't understand."

I exhaled slowly. "I just... I want to be alone right now."

Technically true.

What I didn't say was that I couldn't breathe in this relationship anymore. That I had outgrown it. More importantly, that I had outgrown him. The security I once needed from him was now the thing holding me back.

He sniffed, rubbing his hands over his face. He was spiraling. He apologized for everything. For things he didn't even do. For things he had never done wrong. It wasn't his fault. He was good to me. He loved me.

But the problem was that I just didn't love him anymore.

I should've left it at that and just walked away, let the breakup happen, and give us both space to move on.

Instead, I hesitated. And that hesitation cost me.

Craig saw it.

The way my fingers curled into my lap, the way my eyes dropped to the stairs, the way I wasn't as cold as I wanted to be.

He saw his opening and he took it. He begged, pleaded, and pulled out every memory, every sweet moment, every 'remember when' to remind me what we had. And maybe, for a second, it worked. Maybe it wasn't just nostalgia. Maybe it was guilt. Because Craig was my best friend. And losing him felt bigger than just breaking up.

So I folded. I acquiesced. I let the breakup undo itself within a single day. Hell, a single hour.

And just like that, we stayed together for another year.

———ell———

Craig was a great student. Why is that relevant? Because he was so squeaky clean, so responsible, that even his professors trusted him with their homes when they went out of town. Not a wild college kid. Not someone who'd throw a house party the second the front door closed. No, Craig was the guy who got asked to house-sit.

And for one weekend, in that modest little one-story house, we got a taste of something neither of us had ever experienced before. We played house. Waking up together, making breakfast in a kitchen that wasn't ours. Folding laundry. Falling into an easy rhythm, pretending—just for a little while—that this was real life. That this was our life.

And maybe that's what shifted something in Craig. Because that weekend, he wasn't just the sweet, predictable boyfriend I knew. Something changed. I saw it in his eyes. A different kind of hunger.

Animalistic.

He was bolder. More confident. Like the quiet, well-behaved version of him had been left at the front door, replaced with someone unapologetic in his desire to know me, to learn me.

And that weekend, he explored every single inch of me. Slowly and deliberately. Like he had all the time in the world. Like this was a moment he wanted to memorize.

His lips traced over me with an unhurried certainty, as if he was discovering something new every time he touched me. Across my knee. Up my thigh. He kissed and licked sweet spots that made me yearn for more. He'd kept me in a hypnotic state. Soft and teasing one moment. Firm and knowing the next. And then when I could barely contain my yelps, he went in for the kill. I shivered beneath his kisses. His tongue knew exactly what to do to make me his. Again. And again.

He was more than attentive that weekend. He conquered every square inch of me. Because this wasn't just routine. It wasn't just another night in his dorm room, rushed and quiet and constrained by the walls of a twin-sized bed. This was different. He was different.

And maybe, for a moment, I let myself believe that I could live like this. That I could want this. The comfortable, predictable, quiet life.

The one where we made pancakes in a borrowed kitchen and stole kisses between sips of coffee. Where we collapsed onto the couch, tangled together, completely wrapped up in the ease of it all. Where nothing else existed except us.

By the time the weekend ended, I wasn't sure what had just happened. But something in Craig had awakened. And maybe something in me.

Still wasn't sure if I wanted to keep it.

<hr />

Heartbreak comes in many shapes and sizes. All devastating. All chipping away at your soul. But some, stay with you forever.

My parents were out of town in Hawaii, visiting my sister. That meant I was in charge of feeding and walking the dogs. Also, making sure nothing caught fire, exploded, or otherwise ended in disaster.

I should have taken it seriously. I should have walked them like I was supposed to. But instead, I got lazy.

It was late and I was tired. I'd seen my mom do it a million times, just open the gate and let the dogs roam the neighborhood for a little while. They always came back. Always. So, I let them out. And then, I waited.

Only Cooper returned. Kodiak didn't.

Craig and I waited. Five minutes. Ten. An hour passed.

Still nothing.

Panic started to creep in, cold and unrelenting.

Craig tried to keep me calm. "He's probably just sniffing around," he assured me. "He'll come back when he's ready."

I wanted to believe him. But something felt wrong. So, we got in the car and started driving up and down every street. Our headlights were cutting through the darkness while we called his name over and over.

Nothing.

With every passing minute, my chest got tighter. I prayed. Prayed that when we pulled back into the driveway, Kodiak would be sitting there waiting for us.

But he wasn't.

—————

At 9 p.m., the call came. Animal control. Thank God, they'd found him. He was taken to the emergency vet clinic near my parents' house.

We rushed there, my mind spinning with worry, each minute feeling like an eternity. When I finally saw him, my heart clenched, and tears burned my eyes. He was lying in the kennel, bruised and battered, his brown eyes wide with fear.

The vet said he was shaken, still trembling with fear, but his condition was stable.

"He was hit by a car," she told me gently. "But he's doing okay. We'll keep him for overnight observation, and you can pick him up in the morning."

I nearly collapsed with relief. He was okay. He was hit by a car. *That was fucking terrifying.* But he was going to be okay.

I stroked his fur through the bars of the kennel, whispering apologies. "I'm so sorry, buddy. So sorry. I'll come get you first thing, okay?"

He blinked up at me, his tail giving a weak wag. For the first time that night, I let myself breathe. What a relief.

Well, that relief was short-lived. At 2 a.m., the phone rang again. Kodiak was gone. He died in the middle of the night. Internal bleeding.

I don't even remember what the vet said after that. I hung up the phone. Everything blurred.

I screamed. Loud and guttural and unlike anything that had ever come out of me before. I have never cried and screamed as much as I did in that moment.

Like, ever.

I was crushed. I had killed my childhood dog. I was too lazy to put a damn leash on him. Too busy with unimportant important things to be bothered to take a five-minute walk. I did this. I killed him.

Kodiak was dead. And it was my fault.

Craig tried to console me. He wrapped his arms around me, and held me while I sobbed, while I shook, while I shattered into pieces right there in my childhood home. He whispered soothing words that didn't soothe and he wiped my tears even as more kept falling.

Before I could even think straight, I called Nana. Not my mom. Not my dad. Nana.

My Nana was my everything. My voice of reason. I used to spend summers at her house in Clermont, New York—swimming in her pool until our fingers shriveled and picking cucumbers from her garden like it was our own little world. Whenever life spun out of control, she somehow knew how to steady it again.

And right now, I needed her to do that for me. I needed her to tell me everything was going to be okay the way she used to when I was young.

She picked up on the second ring.

"Sweetheart?"

That one word cracked me open. I couldn't speak. I just cried.

"It's okay," she said softly. "Let it out. I've got you."

And for a moment, I believed her.

Then came the harder part—calling my mother. My hands were shaking so badly I could barely hold the phone as I told her through choked, gasping sobs that I had just killed Kodiak.

Craig was gentle. He was patient and steady, but I think I scared him that night. Up to that point, I had been emotionless.

Quite frankly, I just didn't show a lot of emotion with Craig. I didn't cry much. Didn't argue or fight the way most couples did. Didn't let him take care of me when I was sick.

But this raw, unapologetic devastation. This was traumatizing for him. **And me.**

The floodgates had opened and every single emotion I had bottled up for the entire relationship came pouring out all at once.

Sadness crashed over me, a suffocating wave that left me gasping for air. Devastation hit me hard, a gut punch that knocked the wind out of me. Self-loathing settled deep inside, a dark weight I couldn't shake.

And most of all, **anger** surged through me, like lava racing through my veins, scorching everything in its path.

Most of it was directed at myself. But some of it landed on Craig. Not intentionally. Not at first.

I lashed out, buried in my grief, and he didn't know what to do with that. And even after the grief faded, long after the tears dried, the damage from that night stayed. It was the night that everything snapped.

Because some things, once broken, can't be fixed.

It was the beginning of the end. We didn't break up right then. But that night was a wound we never recovered from.

I don't even know how I met Jared. He was the kind of guy who thought his shit didn't stink. A musician, but not the kind that belonged in some gritty, underground rock band. No, Jared was the type who'd audition for a musical reality TV show and expect to win.

I was still with Craig and things between us had been rocky at best. I had been unhappy for a while and instead of manning up and ending it, I prolonged the inevitable, still scarred by how badly he had taken it the last time I broke up with him.

I let the days pass, hoping maybe, if I just waited long enough, something would change. But nothing changed. I was still done.

And I knew—KNEW—that when I finally ended it, Craig would shatter. He thought I was IT for him. And I knew he wasn't.

Yet, I couldn't handle being the one to destroy him.

So whether it was intentional or unintentional, does it really matter? Because somehow, someway, I still found myself on Jared's couch that night.

It started innocently enough. A group of us hanging out, drinking, talking shit about bands we loved or hated. Jared leaned in, self-assured as hell, smirking in that way that said he already knew where this night was headed. His fingers were strumming absently against his knee like he couldn't stop performing.

"You ever been with a musician?" he asked.

I let out a slow breath, tilting my head. "Can't say that I have."

His smirk widened. "Maybe tonight will be your lucky night."

"Sounds good. Let me know if one shows up," I teased, lifting my eyebrow and searching the room.

This fucker was too cocky for his own good. I found him incredibly off-putting. This guy gave me the ick.

I should've gotten up and walked out. I should have. But I didn't. Instead, I let the moment stretch, let the weight of his stare pull me in. I let my knee brush his while my fingers toyed with the hem of his sleeve like I was considering it.

And who knows, maybe I already was.

Jared leaned in, and his lips touched mine. I let the moment spiral into something I couldn't take back.

The worst part was that my heart wasn't even racing. There were no nerves and no excitement. Just the dull, suffocating realization of my egregious action.

The kiss was sloppy at best. He had to take the lead, which meant he was practically spitting in my mouth.

I was repulsed. By the kiss, or by my behavior—I'm not quite sure. But it was enough. Enough to ruin everything. Enough to make me cross a line I could never uncross.

This wasn't some spur-of-the-moment, heat-of-the-moment, drunk mistake.

This was premeditated.

———

I could have kept it to myself. Could have tucked it away, buried it deep, and carried on like it never happened. But I didn't.

Because maybe I wanted Craig to know. Maybe I knew I was too chickenshit to break up with him outright, so if he found out I cheated, he'd do the dirty work for me. Maybe, deep down, I thought this was my way out.

But that's not exactly how it unfolded.

Later that night, Craig and I sat on the sagging couch in his fraternity house, a couch that had clearly survived too many parties and not enough Febreze. Kind of like our relationship: worn out, stained in places, and long past its prime.

"I don't understand," he whispered. His voice was so small.

I shifted uncomfortably. "I kissed Jared," I repeated, more forceful this time, trying to get a reaction. "I cheated on you."

I braced for impact and rage. For him to call me a whore, throw something, slam a door, do anything to put me in my place. Because that's what I deserved.

But Craig just looked at me. His face didn't twist in anger or harden with resentment. It didn't snap into the fight I had mentally prepared for. And then, his face crumpled and his eyes filled with tears.

Goddammit.

"So, I guess this means we're done," I said, sadness creeping into my voice despite everything.

"Wait, what?" he said, his voice small, shaky. "Please don't do this."

I blinked at him, heart hardening.

"Craig, come on. We're breaking up. I cheated."

But he shook his head, frantic now. And then, the worst part. Instead of yelling or walking away. He begged.

"No, we don't have to. We can fix this. I forgive you, okay? Please don't leave me. Please."

I swallowed. I had expected rage. I had prepared for pain. But I had not prepared for this – for forgiveness. For him to look at me like I was still something worth keeping.

I stared at his puffy, tear-streaked face, at the way he was still reaching for me, still believing in us, still believing in ME. And I caved.

AGAIN.

I know I should have ended it right there. I should have stuck to my words, stood my ground, told him no, this is done, we're over. But instead, I saw him shaking. Saw him falling apart. And once again, I chickened out. I stayed.

Even though I knew I was done and that I'd never look at him the same way again. In that moment, I lost the last bit of respect I had for him.

And for myself.

I didn't stay because I wanted to, I stayed because I was too much of a coward to leave. I stayed because I didn't know how to be the bad guy and I knew that if I walked out that door, Craig would break into a million pieces. And I didn't want to be the one who had to watch him shatter.

That night, I let him hold me and press his face into my neck, whispering that everything was going to be okay.

"Yeah," I murmured. "It's gonna be okay."

Because deep down, I already knew it wasn't.

So, I lied through my teeth one last time.

—— *ele* ——

The night I finally ended it for good was a tough night. It had been about four months since the Jared debacle—four months of trying to move past it, of pretending we could make it work, and of me lying to myself.

This particular night, we went out to dinner. And for the first time in a long time, I actually felt hopeful about us.

I even told my mother earlier that day, "I think I could end up with Craig."

Because he was safe and he loved me, and as a result, I had convinced myself that love should be enough.

By that point, we'd been together for nearly three years. We had just graduated, and big life changes loomed ahead. I'd moved back in with my parents while waiting for my new apartment to be ready, and Craig had stayed local instead of moving back to New York. Probably for me.

Neither of us said it, but we both knew things were different now.

We got into an argument—a rare thing for us. Maybe that's why it felt so heavy. Ever since Jared, there had been this quiet, suffocating tension between us. Neither of us ever admitted it, but it was always there. And that night, we stopped pretending it wasn't.

Craig drove me home. I remember sitting there in the passenger seat, staring out the window, feeling that awful weight settle in my chest. When we pulled into the driveway, he put the car in park but didn't move to shut it off.

I could feel him looking at me, like he knew—like he felt it too. The quiet unraveling. The slow, steady fall apart. But neither of us said anything.

He followed me inside and up to my room, where we sat, watching TV and pretending everything was normal. Except it wasn't. Because the argument from earlier wasn't finished.

The conversation picked back up and it was tense, clipped, but mostly, fragile. And suddenly, I felt so damn tired. Tired of forcing it and pretending. And above all, tired of dragging this relationship out.

I turned to him, and before I could talk myself out of it, the words slipped past my lips.

"Craig, I'm so sorry, but we're done."

The air shifted. His entire face crumpled and just like so many times before, he begged. He pleaded with me, told me he loved me and told me we could fix this. Tears spilled down his face and something inside me snapped.

Because this time was different. This time, I didn't waver. I didn't second-guess myself and I didn't give in. I stayed quiet.

But most importantly, I stayed strong.

I watched as he broke in front of me, his hands trembling as he struggled to understand how we had gotten here, trying to convince me it wasn't over.

And the worst part is that I felt nothing. Just... emptiness.

Like all the love, all the guilt, all the hesitation had drained out of me long before this moment. Craig just didn't know it yet.

Eventually, he stood, his shoulders slumped in defeat, his face was wet with tears, and his hands still shaking. He hugged me before walking out of the house. Broken.

I stood there, frozen, listening to the front door close.

He was gone and it was really over.

⁓

He took part of my heart with him that night.

Not because I still loved him, but because I never wanted to be the person who crushed him. I never wanted to be the reason someone doubted love.

And yet, that's exactly what I had done. I had toyed with his emotions and strung him along for far too long.

I was ashamed of myself. I was a horrible human being.

Well, karma is a motherfucker.

Bobby: The Whirlwind Romance

"I can tell there was an accident – Saosin"

Monday.

E ven though I had a 9 to 5, I also worked part-time at a local radio station. The perks were free concerts, backstage passes, and meeting bands. But the one glaringly obvious downside? The on-air personalities.

I was working the promotions table at a dueling piano bar one night when *he* walked in wearing a black hoodie, camo cargos, black socks, and multi-colored Etnies. His red-and-black faux hawk peeked out from beneath his hood, and something about him screamed trouble—the fun kind. I could only imagine the sleeves of tattoos hidden under that hoodie, waiting for my adoration.

Tattooed, confident, and—let's be honest—exactly my type of mistake.

"You don't see that every day," he said casually.

I blinked. "What?"

He gestured vaguely toward me. "Business casual with black nail polish. It's a bold aesthetic."

I followed his gaze to my button-up blouse and pencil skirt, then down to my chipped black nails. Ah, my day job was still clinging to me, and apparently, it was making a statement.

I looked back up at him, suddenly hyper-aware of the way he stood, completely at ease like he'd walked in expecting to own the place. His confidence was borderline cocky, but not in a way that made me want to roll my eyes. Instead, I wanted to match it.

He spoke like we already knew each other, like he wasn't a total stranger walking up to me with zero hesitation.

"Yeah," I said, half amused. "Gotta keep people guessing."

He tilted his head, intrigued. "What exactly are you keeping people guessing about? Whether you're here for tequila or to assess their credit score?"

He chuckled, the sound deep and effortless. Proud of himself.

Was he flirting? And now, I'd left the conversation in an awkward pause.

Think of something witty. Something sharp but charming. Whatever you do, don't revert to insulting him. You can play nice. There is no need to snap the back of his bra, metaphorically of course. Flirt back. Please, just be friendly. Don't insult him.

"Well," I said, tapping my chin. "At least I'm not the poster child for some whining emo punk band."

Aaand there it is. Blown.

He paused. A long pause.

Then, instead of walking away, he grinned ear to ear. Like he loved it.

"I'm Bobby," he said, flashing a grin and extending his hand.

"Sam." I shook his hand, firm grip, solid eye contact. If he was testing me, I wasn't about to blink first.

And just like that, the game was on. We talked the rest of the night. About art, our jobs, our lives, but mostly, music. That was the drug. We tested each other's knowledge on hardcore bands, underground bands, the up-and-comers. He could keep up and I was impressed.

And then I found out the kicker—he was an on-air personality for the rock station. A DJ. My actual nightmare.

"I hadn't seen you around the station before," I said, narrowing my eyes.

"Day job," he shrugged. "I'm a Financial Planner."

I blinked. "Wait, you're an on-air rock DJ and a financial planner?"

"Multi-faceted," he said, cocky as hell.

Dangerous.

And for the first time in a very, very long time, I left a bar feeling giddy. I was completely intrigued by this new man. Off balance, in a way I hadn't felt in years.

Because this wasn't just attraction. It was a full-body reaction. And that scared the hell out of me in the best way possible.

———ele———

Wednesday.

I pulled up to a massive wooden house on the water. Actually, I'm not even sure you could call this a house, it was five houses stitched together, Frankenstein-style, into one sprawling testament to privilege.

Bobby had asked me to swing by his friend's place so we could hang out. And now, I was here.

His crew was friendly enough. They were curious about the tall girl with the sarcastic wit who had apparently caught Bobby's attention. All except for one.

Enter Spike. Tall, lanky, bleached-blond spikes frozen in place with enough gel to supply a third-world country. His entire vibe screamed arrogant prick, but you could sense his insecurity, wondering if it was his personality or daddy's money-keeping people around. He was staring me down like I was an unwanted house-guest who had already overstayed her welcome.

"She's cute," one of Bobby's friends said, grinning in my direction.

Spike exhaled dramatically, crossing his arms. "Bobby, dude, she's just some random girl, and you invited her to my house."

Oh. *Ohhhh. I did not like this one.*

Bobby immediately draped an arm around me, pulling me in just a little too close. A statement.

It sent a jolt through my system, a full-body reaction I couldn't stop if I tried. I felt the heat rush from my toes to my eyelashes. Goosebumps bloomed across my skin. And Bobby noticed. His lips quirked into a knowing smile, and that's when it hit me. Crap. He already knows the effect he has on me. This was going to end badly.

After about 20 minutes of awkward small talk and subtle glares from Spike, Bobby grabbed my hand.

"Let's get out of here."

No argument from me.

We walked outside, the air thick with summer humidity, the sound of cicadas buzzing from the trees. He stopped beside my car and turned to me with a knowing smirk. "Let's just get this over with."

I blinked. His hand slid into the front pocket of his hoodie, and he took a slow step forward, closing the space between us.

I barely had time to process his words before his hand cupped the side of my face, his thumb grazed my cheekbone, and his fingers threaded into my hair at the nape of my neck. It was deliberate—controlled, yet unhurried—like he'd already decided exactly how this was going to play out.

His breath was warm against my lips, and my pulse pounded so loud I was sure he could hear it. The butterflies in my stomach were in overdrive, threatening to escape.

And then, finally, he kissed me. Soft at first, like he was tasting the moment before claiming it. The slow drag of his lips against mine sent heat pooling low in my stomach. His other hand slid around my waist, pulling me closer until there was nothing between us but the night air and the unbearable tension we'd been dancing around all evening.

I let out the smallest gasp, and that was all the invitation he needed.

The second kiss was deeper, more urgent. My hands fisted into the fabric of his hoodie, and I felt him smile against my lips. His fingers tightened at the base of my neck, tilting my head to deepen the kiss, and—holy hell—I was in trouble.

When he finally pulled back, his forehead rested against mine, and I could still feel the ghost of his lips on mine. My eyes were still closed, lips still parted, still wanting.

He chuckled softly.

"Yep," he murmured, voice low and satisfied. "That's what I thought."

I opened my eyes, breathless. Smug Bastard.

He opened the car door for me, and I barely remembered how to sit. I started driving down the road, my hands gripping the wheel like I needed an anchor. I pulled into an empty parking lot, threw the car in park, and turned to him.

"What do you want to do?" I asked, my voice not nearly as steady as I wanted it to be.

He stretched, leaning back in the seat, grinning.

"We could go see a movie or something?"

We did not go see a movie. We stayed in that car, parked on an empty street for three hours.

Talking. Kissing. Talking. Kissing. Again. And again.

I learned so much about him that night—his past, his dreams, his wounds. Bobby's last relationship had ended two feet away from an engagement ring. His girlfriend of five years had looked him in the eyes one morning and simply said, "I don't love you anymore."

And then, she was gone. He was blindsided and wrecked. My take? She was absolutely boning someone else. But I kept that opinion to myself.

"I don't know why I'm telling you all this," he admitted, shaking his head.

"I barely know you. Yet, I *want* to tell you. It's weird."

I understood completely. For some reason, people had always spilled their deepest, darkest secrets to me. I was a sponge for oversharing, soaked in tea I never asked to sip. However, in this instance, I didn't mind.

"I've broken someone's heart before," I admitted. "It took me over a year to finally find the courage to end it."

Bobby listened. Really listened. It was like he was memorizing every word, watching my lips move, like if he missed a single sentence, the whole thing would shatter.

We were completely in tune. It sounds cliché, because it was. But that night, we knew, this wasn't just a fling. It wasn't casual. It was something.

And that something was about to consume me.

Friday.

The charity benefit we were attending that night was for a local girl battling bacterial meningitis. That local girl happened to be my former best friend. But that's a different heartbreak altogether—another story for another time.

I opened the door and nearly lost my balance. Bobby stood there, wearing a black t-shirt and perfectly fitted black jeans. The outfit clung to him just enough, like it had been tailored with the sole purpose of destroying me. And those mesmerizing tattoos were on display, and like a kid in a candy store, I couldn't wait to touch them.

He looked like the drummer of a screamo rock band. And I wanted to lick the skin off his body and also check his playlist to make sure it wasn't just Death Cab and breakup ballads.

"Jesus Christ," I blurted out.

His lips quirked. "That a compliment?"

Before I could answer, he wrapped his arms around my waist and kissed me. Right there, on my damn porch. Not a casual peck. Not a *Hey, good to see you* kiss. A full-body, melt-into-each-other, people-slowing-down-on-the-sidewalk-to-watch-us type of kiss.

I hadn't even invited him in yet. I didn't care.

—ело—

We arrived hand in hand. I introduced Bobby to my friends, expecting him to be a little out of place, but he wasn't. Not even a little. He adapted effortlessly, sliding into conversations, cracking jokes, managing to be both charming and completely attentive to me at the same time. It was unsettling.

"You've got it bad," my best friend, Georgia, whispered in my ear.

Before I could roll my eyes, she added, "But so does he."

I frowned. "You think?"

"I've never seen a guy look at a girl the way he looks at you," she said.

I snorted. "Ease up on the Lifetime movies, bird."

"Fine, all I'm saying is he's gonna put his P in your V TONIGHT!"

"You're ridiculous," I laughed.

But I couldn't stop myself. I looked over at Bobby and he was already watching me. Like he'd been doing it all night and he hadn't stopped. We stared at each other. It should have been awkward but it wasn't.

Then, because I have the emotional depth of a toddler, I made it into a staring war. *First person to blink gets bitch-slapped.*

Kidding. Mostly.

But that lingering look was enough. I knew it. And he knew I knew it.

We were completely intrigued with one another and couldn't stop smiling. More importantly, we couldn't hide our feelings for one another. It was very vulnerable on both our parts.

We left the benefit and went back to my house. Yes, my best friend is an absolute psychic. I don't know what possessed me that night. Maybe it was his cologne or the way his lip ring glinted in the dim light of my car. Or maybe, just maybe, I was already gone.

I grabbed his hand and led him straight to my bedroom. No hesitation. No second-guessing. Just him and me and the undeniable weight of what was about to happen.

Bobby kissed me slowly at first. It was soft, like he was testing the waters. Then, not soft at all. The second my fingers curled into his hair, his body went from patient to frantic, like he'd been holding himself back and had finally given in.

And boy did I want that—the rush, the urgency. I wanted to feel like he needed me as much as I suddenly, overwhelmingly, needed him. So when his hands gripped my waist and pulled me onto his lap, I didn't hesitate. I let my head fall back, let him take over, let myself get completely lost in the way his hands ran down my back, the way his breath hitched every time I moved against him.

It was chaotic and messy. And when his mouth trailed from my lips to my jaw, down my neck, I stopped thinking altogether. Somewhere between grinding on his lap and my dress hiking up my thighs, he stood, lifting me with him, and I let out a gasp, which immediately turned into a startled laugh when my back hit the mattress.

I was buzzing with anticipation, my skin flushed, and a bit breathless. My body hummed with energy, every nerve alive. I reached for him, my hands trembling slightly, but before I could close the distance, he was already on me.

And it was... fast.

Really fast.

Like *we have 90 seconds before the house burns down* kind of fast. Like *this should have been the trailer before the actual movie* kind of fast.

I barely had time to register anything before it was over. Bobby collapsed next to me, chest heaving, satisfied as hell. And me, well, I was less satisfied.

Honestly, I had no idea how to feel. I could have sat there, analyzing the moment. Could have admitted that it wasn't exactly mind-blowing. But instead, I turned my head to look at him. And he was already looking at me, like I was the best thing that had ever happened to him. Like he couldn't believe I was real.

And that was enough. So I smiled. And I let myself believe it had been amazing. Because sometimes, when you *really* like someone...

You can rationalize a four-inch penis.

Because everything else about that night was perfect. The way he kissed and touched me, as if he was memorizing me. The way his body molded against mine, fitting in ways that shouldn't have felt as natural as they did. The way he stared into my eyes, even after, when we lay tangled in the sheets like he was trying to figure me out.

And maybe the worst part was the way he held me until morning. I woke up in his arms and stayed there, frozen. I should've moved. I should've started pulling back, but the truth was I was in too deep.

But instead, I let it happen. I let *him* happen.

Talking, kissing, touching, and existing in a bubble where nothing else mattered.

It was official. I was already too far gone.

—ell—

Saturday.

Bobby and I spent the entire day together, which at this point, felt normal.

Natural. Like we'd been doing this for months, not days.

By the time evening rolled around, we met up with his friends for pizza at some hole-in-the-wall joint that looked one health inspection away from being condemned. The kind of place where the booths stuck to your skin in the summer, and the only thing colder than the beer was the guy behind the counter who didn't even pretend to like his job.

It wasn't fancy and it wasn't trying too hard, which is probably why I leaned into Bobby a little harder.

I wanted to be here with him and his friends, even though they were still trying to figure me out.

We all crowded into a rickety booth in the back, a pitcher of beer already sweating onto the table. Bobby didn't leave my side. Not for a second. I caught the glances from his friends—assessing me, sizing me up. Was I just another girl? Or was I something else?

And maybe that's why I kept my arm draped over his, kept my legs crossed toward him, made sure my laughter was just a little louder when he was the one talking. Because I needed them to know, I wasn't just another girl, I was his girl.

Bobby's friends were exactly what you'd expect. A little too confident, a little too opinionated, and way too entertained by Bobby's love life.

There was Brandon—a six-foot-five teddy bear with a permanent smirk and a deep appreciation for whiskey.

Then there was Tom, who looked like he should've been in a band but couldn't play a single instrument. His talents were starting shit and probably dodging commitment.

And then, of course, Spike—Bobby's human red flag of a best friend. Spike was the kind of guy who always had something to prove. To himself, to women, to the universe. Frankly, if I hadn't already been obsessed with Bobby, I might have been tempted to spar with him just for fun.

Instead, I spent the night wrapped in Bobby's arm, leaning into him at every opportunity.

At some point, I excused myself to go to the bathroom. The place was relatively quiet for a Saturday night with the scent of melted cheese and cheap beer thick in the air. Yet, there was still a line for the women's restroom. Of course, there was a line. There is always a line.

I leaned against the peeling door frame, zoning out until I heard my name.

"Sam is badass," Brandon said.

"She's way too hot for you," Tom added with a snicker.

I chuckled. *As if I hadn't heard that before.*

But it was Bobby's response that made my breath catch.

"Relax, it's not like she's my girlfriend. And don't hate 'cause you haven't graduated from dating tweens yet."

They all laughed. And I should have laughed, too. I should have recognized it for what it was, a joke, a deflection, just boys being boys. But it didn't feel like a joke. It felt like a line drawn in permanent marker between what we were and what we'd never be.

Because in that moment, he wasn't claiming me. He wasn't saying, *She's different. She's not just some hookup.* He was confirming that I was temporary.

And, to be clear, he wasn't wrong, I wasn't his girlfriend. I was just the girl who wanted to be.

I shouldn't have cared. Maybe I should've matched his casual with my own, but I was already all in. Heart, hope, delusion—fully invested, over here. And I was desperate to believe he was, too.

So I swallowed it and tucked the doubt into the same mental drawer where I kept my other ignored red flags. Right next to *this isn't going anywhere and you deserve better.*

And when I came back to the table, Bobby pulled me onto his lap and kissed me like he hadn't seen me in weeks. Like I was the only girl in the world.

And I let myself believe it.

Sunday.

The next morning, Bobby was already at the station, working the Sunday morning shift, which meant, for the first time in days, I wasn't with him.

It felt weird, like something was off-balance.

I rolled out of bed, threw on a hoodie and leggings, and decided retail therapy was the solution. The mall would be a solid distraction. A mindless and loud place where I could wander through stores, pretend to care about things like candles and overpriced handbags, and not overanalyze every second of this whirlwind romance.

I drove to the mall, half-distracted, half-hungover on Bobby. Yesterday had been perfect—pizza, beers, his arm around me, the way he had pulled me onto his lap like I was his. But then there was the other part. The part where he'd let his friends talk about me like I was just some girl. Where he hadn't defended me and just laughed along.

And I hated that I cared. I hated that one tiny moment of doubt was eating away at all the good ones.

But then, Bobby's voice filled my car. I had the radio on out of habit, the rock station humming in the background as I idled at a red light. His voice was smooth and confident through my speakers. I should have melted and soaked it in. But instead, I braced myself for impact.

"Dudes, I'm super happy. I'm on a high. You know that feeling, don't you?"

I blinked at the road, grip tightening on the wheel. *A high?*

"You know when you meet a girl that is cooler than you'd ever expect," he continued.

Ah. A high over a girl. I felt it immediately—the anxiety creeping in. Because what if it wasn't me? What if I wasn't the girl making him feel like this? What if he'd met someone else and I was just another name on a list?

My stomach flipped.

I mean, yeah, we had spent nearly every single day together since we met. Yeah, he slept in my bed and kissed me like he needed me to breathe. But that didn't mean he wasn't still playing the field.

I wasn't his girlfriend. He declared that last night. And as much as I wanted to believe I was different, was I really?

My heart hammered against my ribcage.

And, as expected, he put all of my worries at ease.

"This next song's about a girl named Sam," Bobby continued.

A girl named Sam.

Me.

Holy. Shit.

I exhaled so hard that my entire body sagged into the seat. A rush
of relief, followed by the kind of giddy hysteria that made my
fingertips tingle. God, I was insane. For even doubting him. For
even letting my brain take me there.

I pulled into the mall parking lot, cut the engine, and just sat there
grinning like an absolute idiot.

He was on the air. And he was talking about me.

Bobby was cool, loved, and listened to by thousands of people, and
he had just told all of them that I was the girl making him happy.

And just like that, I was back. If I wasn't already spiraling into
full-fledged infatuation mode, I was now free-falling. No more
doubt or questioning. Just Bobby and this feeling that I didn't
want to end.

I didn't even realize I was still sitting there until my phone vibrated
with a text.

Bobby: *Did you hear?*

Oh, I heard.

And I was completely, utterly, no-turning-back done for.

Monday.

I hadn't gone to work that morning, but not because I was sick. At least, not in the way that counted. I felt off. Like my body was too slow, too heavy, too aware of the fact that I had spent the last week drowning in Bobby and now, for the first time, he wasn't here.

It was pathetic. I knew it was pathetic. But I still spent the morning checking my phone more times than I'd ever admit out loud.

So when the doorbell rang and I opened it to find him standing there grinning like he'd been waiting for this moment all day, I didn't know whether to slam the door or throw myself at him. It was stupidly satisfying.

"I missed you," he said, stepping inside, wrapping his arms around me like he belonged there.

And maybe he did.

"No complaints here," I murmured into his chest, inhaling his scent, already forgetting whatever unease had settled in my stomach that morning.

He pulled back just enough to look at me. The kind of look that made you feel like the only girl in the world.

"You look beautiful," he gushed.

I let out a short laugh. "In yoga pants and a hoodie?"

"Absolutely."

And then he kissed me. Not a soft, thoughtful kiss. Not an I-just-stopped-by-to-see-you kiss. A kiss that tasted like promise and made me believe that maybe, just maybe, I hadn't been crazy to fall so fast.

We walked up and down my street, hand in hand, like a couple that had been doing this for years. It was too easy. Too effortless. And maybe that's why I ignored every warning sign.

"I've never met anyone like you," Bobby said, his thumb brushing against mine as we walked. "You're funny and smart and I find myself thinking about you nonstop."

His voice was soft and honest.

"It's hard to concentrate because you're on my mind all the time," he continued.

I should have said something snarky. I should have kept it light. But I didn't, because I wanted to hear what came next.

"I hadn't fully recovered from my ex-girlfriend before I met you. And now," He squeezed my hand. "You're all I can think about."

I swallowed hard. Those words should have set off alarms. I should have heard the warning hidden beneath them. But I was too far gone.

"I feel stronger for you in these few days than I ever had for her in the years we were together."

I stopped walking and looked at him.

Years.

He had spent *years* loving this girl.

And now, I was supposed to believe that after a few days, I'd eclipsed all of that. I should have questioned it. Should have said something, anything, to ground us back in reality. But I didn't. Instead, I squeezed his hand back and let myself believe every word. This was dangerous and completely, and utterly, reckless.

I should've seen the red flag whipping me in the face but I couldn't, I had fallen for him too. He was amazing and my senses and rationale were completely clouded by his charisma. To be honest, I hadn't felt this way about someone ever. Not even with Craig.

And this was exactly what I wanted. Because Bobby wasn't just playing the part of the perfect guy. He was saying everything I wanted to hear. And I was eating it up.

We were both just out of long-term relationships and had found one another. We were both on the same page.

Or so I thought.

Tuesday.

Tuesday night we found ourselves at a dive bar with his friends.

The kind of place with slick floors, cheap drinks, and a playlist that alternated between 2000s throwbacks and bass-heavy remixes.

For most of the night, the music was blaring—loud enough to drown out thoughts I didn't want to have anyway. Thoughts about how fast this was moving and how dangerous it felt to like someone this much, this quickly. I was already picturing what it would be like to meet his parents, like some delusional Stepford wife.

But then, the music paused. Maybe the DJ took a smoke break, or divine intervention decided I needed clarity. I was sitting at the bar, shoulder to shoulder with Bobby, his arm slung lazily around my chair. I was his, that's what this touch said. That's what I liked believing, anyway. And then some random suit in a polo and slacks slid up next to me, leaning on the bar like he was about to do me the favor of a lifetime.

"Can I buy you a drink?" he asked, completely ignoring Bobby's existence.

I didn't hesitate. "No, thanks."

I thought that would be the end of it. But men like this don't like being told no.

He immediately noticed Bobby's hand on my shoulder. Instead
of walking away, he gave Bobby a once-over, scrunching his
nose like Bobby was some kind of sub-par selection off a menu.

"You're way too hot for that weirdo."

Bobby tensed beside me, but before he could say a word, I
turned in my seat, already bristling.

"Come again?" I said sharply.

"Oh, I can make you come all night," the prick responded.

Bobby leaned forward then, his usual easy confidence replaced
with something edgier.

"You can fuck right off, Country Club."

The guy laughed like Bobby was some joke he hadn't finished
telling yet. And then he asked, smug as hell, "Did you even go
to college? Better yet, did you graduate high school? I bet you
don't even know the Pythagorean Theorem. Let's start small,
can you recite the alphabet?" he droned on, clearly enamored
with the sound of his voice.

And that's when I saw it, the flicker of something behind
Bobby's eyes. A moment of hesitation, or insecurity. Like a tiny
part of him still believed he had something to prove. So, before
he could even open his mouth—

"$A^2 + B^2 = C^2$," I quickly responded. "I have a Master's degree, Motherfucker. And here's a pop quiz for you. Does this bullshit typically work on women or will you be heading home alone to jerk off to a syndicated episode of the Golden Girls?"

The guy blinked at me. I smiled sweetly.

Bobby let out a low chuckle, eyes darting to me like he was both amused and impressed.

Country Club just stared at me for a beat, then let out an annoyed huff, rolling his eyes as he turned back to the bar, grabbed his beer, and walked away, calling me a bitch under his breath.

Bobby's fingers tightened on my shoulder. I could feel the tension thrumming through him, the way his jaw was still locked tight.

And just like that, the night changed.

We were out celebrating Mardi Gras, drinks in hand, his friends laughing, music pulsing but Bobby wasn't the same. Though he still held his arm around me, something felt off. Like he was going through the motions but wasn't really there. Like my quick defense had done more damage than good.

At some point, when the conversation was in full swing, I leaned into him, my lips grazing his ear.

"Is everything okay?"

He exhaled sharply. "Just having a bad day."

A bad day. Right. That's what this was.

I could have pushed. I could have called bullshit. But I didn't. I shrugged it off, didn't persist or question it.

Because deep down, I knew what was coming, and I wanted to pretend that this was all a fairytale that could come true.

It wasn't.

～ℓℓ～

Wednesday.

After the Mardi Gras dive bar incident, I told myself Bobby was just in a mood. Everyone has bad days. Maybe he was stressed or felt insecure about the whole Pythagorean theorem thing, even though that guy totally deserved to be put in his place.

Maybe, maybe, maybe. I was really great at *maybes*.

And that's why, when I saw him the next night, I still let myself believe we were fine.

Bobby had a radio promo event that night at a bar downtown. I wasn't planning on going. It wasn't my scene, and I hated the overly flirty girls who draped themselves over DJs like they were rock stars instead of guys who talked into microphones for a living.

But when I hadn't heard from him all day—when my texts went unread, when my stomach started twisting itself into a panic—I decided, *fuck it*. I wasn't about to sit in my apartment overthinking myself into a breakdown.

So, I went.

I should have stayed home.

The bar was packed. Radio interns were scattered everywhere, handing out station swag—t-shirts, bottle openers, neon bracelets that glowed under the dim bar lights. A group of college girls huddled, giggling in anticipation, clearly hoping for *their moment* with Bobby.

And then there he was. Sitting at the promo table, headphones around his neck, talking into the mic for a live broadcast. He looked fine to me. Normal, even. Like nothing was wrong and he hadn't ignored me all day. Like I wasn't standing there, right in front of him, waiting for him to notice me.

Then, finally, his eyes met mine and something was off. His expression was unreadable. There was no easy grin, no warmth, just a flicker of something I couldn't quite place before he forced a smile that didn't quite meet his eyes and looked away.

Away. Like I was just another face in the crowd.

I felt my stomach drop, my fingers curling around the strap of my purse as I hesitated. My body screamed at me to go to him and close the distance. To pretend like everything was okay. My brain on the other hand screamed at me to go home. This was a horrible idea. I had my proof that the lack of response all day was intentional. Leave. Literally, run as fast as you can.

But I didn't. Instead, I moved toward the bar, ordered a drink, and waited. He'd come to me. Of course, he would.

Except, he didn't. An hour passed. He never came over. I watched as he laughed with the promo team, high-fived the bartenders, and hugged some girl I didn't recognize, his hands lingering on her waist just a little too long.

I wasn't the jealous type. But I also wasn't blind. And this wasn't the Bobby who had confessed that I was all he thought about. This was someone else. Someone slipping away.

Still, I waited. And then, finally, as the night wound down, he walked over. But instead of pulling me into him, instead of pressing his lips to my lips like he always did, he just stood there, hands in his pockets. A stiff, unreadable expression on his face.

"You're here," he said like it was a mild inconvenience.

My stomach twisted. "Yeah. Thought I'd surprise you."

"Cool."

...Cool? That's it?

No *hey baby*, no *I missed you*, no *I love seeing you here*. Just cool.

The air between us stretched uncomfortably. I searched his face for some kind of explanation. A crack in his armor. A clue.

Nothing.

"Is that alright?" I asked, forcing lightness into my tone.

"Yeah, just have to put on a show and be someone else when I'm out representing the station," he responded.

Hmm, interesting take given that he professed to all of his listeners not 3 days prior, that a girl named Sam made him incredibly happy. Now, he needed to put on a show to those same listeners and present an alter ego.

Noted.

"Everything okay?" I asked,

He exhaled, rubbing the back of his neck. "Just tired. Long day. I'm gonna head out."

Long day. Right. It wasn't me. It wasn't us. He was just *tired*.

I forced a smile, nodded, and let it slide, even though my gut was screaming at me not to.

And then, without another word, Bobby leaned in, kissed my cheek—*not my lips*—and walked away. Not back to work. Not to wrap up the event. But straight out the front door.

I sat there, frozen. Watching the door swing shut behind him. Feeling the first real crack form in my chest.

~elle~

Thursday.

I knew it the moment he walked in.

There was something in his posture, the way he carried himself, like he was holding something back. His eyes wouldn't quite meet mine, as if avoiding the truth we both knew. And before he even opened his mouth, my stomach dropped, a wave of dread crashing over me.

Bobby sat down on my bed, hands clasped, elbows on his knees, staring down at the floor like if he just focused hard enough, maybe the right words would come.

I stood there, arms crossed, a sick, desperate hope clawing at my chest—maybe this isn't what I think it is.

But it was.

"I'm sorry," he said, voice quiet, careful, rehearsed. "I need to clear my head. My parents are getting a divorce and I can't handle a girlfriend right now."

It should have hit all at once, like a wrecking ball to my ribcage. But instead, it was slow, suffocating, like trying to swim against a rip current. One minute, you're fighting to keep your head above water, and the next, you're drowning.

I sat down beside him, my mind grasping for logic. For reason. Shit, for something to make this make sense.

"I don't understand," I said, my voice too even. "You said you felt strongly about me. How does that just... disappear?"

"It hasn't," he insisted. "I just have other things on my mind right now."

Bullshit.

I didn't say it, but I thought it so loudly that I was sure he could hear it. This wasn't about his parents or timing, for that matter. This was about fear. He was afraid of how much he felt for me, and instead of leaning into it, he ran.

"Honestly, I've fallen for you, and that scares me," he admitted.

There it was. The confession and admission I clung to. But what did it even matter? Falling for me didn't stop him from leaving.

My eyes burned. I felt the wetness against my cheeks before I even realized the tears had fallen.

Bobby exhaled sharply. "I'm so sorry."

And then he left.

—ele—

Recap, because my brain refused to compute.

Monday: We flirted.

Wednesday: We kissed.

Friday: We made love.

Saturday: He professed his love.

Wednesday: He pushed me away.

Thursday: He broke my fucking heart.

—ele—

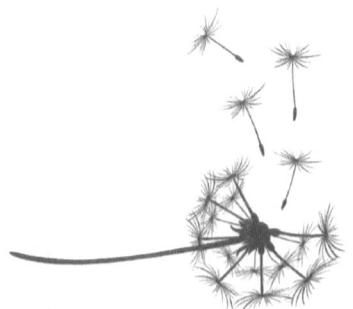

Friday.

I woke up to silence.

No text. No call. No good morning, beautiful.

Just... nothing.

I laid there, staring at my ceiling, with a gaping hole in my chest. The night before had been a blur. After Bobby left, I sat in my room for what felt like hours, replaying every conversation, every kiss, every touch, trying to pinpoint the exact moment when everything shifted.

Why did I ignore the signs? Had I pushed too hard? Was I too much?

The questions chased each other in my head, a never-ending cycle of self-doubt that made it impossible to sleep.

By the time the sun rose, I felt hollow. I told myself I wouldn't text him. I lasted two hours.

Me: *I miss you.*

I stared at the screen, willing the three little dots to appear, but they didn't.

I threw myself into distractions. Anything to keep my mind occupied. But no matter how hard I tried, Bobby was everywhere.

Every song that played on the radio station. Every couple I passed on the street. Every fucking guy with a hoodie and tattoos. All of it was a fucking reminder.

Even my goddamn shampoo smelled like him. I considered burning my apartment down just to rid myself of his ghost. Instead, I settled for drinking my weight in Captain and Cokes.

My friends tried to keep me sane. Georgia, in particular, had gone full war mode.

"I swear to GOD, Sam, if you text him again, I will throw your phone into the ocean."

I nodded solemnly. "You're right. I won't."

I texted him anyway.

Me: *This sucks.*
Me: *I hate this.*
Me: *I hate you.*

I deleted the last one before it sent.

Maybe that was progress.

I tried to be there for him, to support him through his parents' divorce, to be the person he could lean on when everything else in his life felt like it was falling apart. Or so he had said to me.

My friends told me I was crazy. They saw through his bullshit in ways I refused to. They told me to move on, and stop waiting, because he was never coming back.

But how could I? He told me he had never felt this way about anyone before and that he had fallen for me. How do feelings like that just disappear? Mine certainly hadn't.

So I convinced myself he just needed time, I could wait, and be his shoulder to cry on.

But Bobby didn't want a shoulder. Bobby didn't want me.

———

I shouldn't have gone out that night. I knew it the second I stepped into the bar. Too many memories. Too many places where I had sat with Bobby, laughed with Bobby, kissed Bobby.

I was already half drunk when I saw him across the room, laughing and flirting with some girl pressed against his side, whispering in his ear.

I wanted to throw up. Or throw myself into oncoming traffic. Instead, I made the worst decision of all. I let him see me.

His eyes flicked to mine, and for a second—just a second—something softened.

Then, just like that, he looked away.

And I broke.

I stormed past Georgia, past the crowd, past the bouncers, straight out into the cold night air, gasping for breath like I had been sucker-punched in the ribs.

Georgia found me minutes later, arms crossed.

"Let's get the fuck out of here."

"I'm fine."

"I know," she lied.

I wiped my face, realizing for the first time that I had been crying.

I wasn't fine. Not even a little.

<center>~~~</center>

I stayed in bed for a week. I didn't eat, barely moved, and just lay there, my body aching in ways that had nothing to do with physical pain. The kind of ache that settles into your bones, like grief with nowhere to go.

I had never truly understood heartbreak until now. It wasn't just sadness. It was exhaustion and grief. It was carrying the weight of someone who was still alive but no longer belonged to you. And that kind of weight doesn't just sit on your chest, it crushes it.

The truth is, I thought I knew what heartbreak felt like. But the only version of it I'd ever experienced before Bobby came from a ten-year-old girl named Liza.

In fourth grade, she was my first best friend. For two years we were inseparable. Matching friendship bracelets, inside jokes, whispering about boy bands and making grand plans for our future like ten-year-olds do when they're convinced they'll never be apart.

And then we moved. Again.

Two years later, when I finally moved back, I walked into our classroom expecting everything to snap back into place like it had before.

Instead, Liza ignored me completely. No smile. No wave. No acknowledgment that I even existed. And just like that, everyone else followed her lead. It was as if I had been erased.

For a week I tried to figure out what I had done wrong. Then I stopped trying.

My mom transferred me to another school not long after, but the damage was done. That was the first time I had ever felt my chest crack open like that. The first time someone I loved looked at me like I was nothing.

I thought that was heartbreak. Turns out, I had no idea what heartbreak actually felt like.

Because Liza disappearing from my life hurt. Bobby demolished my heart, and I had no clue how I'd recover from that level of pain.

My mom called. I let it ring. Georgia showed up. I hid under the covers and prayed she'd think I wasn't home. Because even comfort felt too heavy to hold.

But eventually, I caved.

Me: *How are you doing with your parents divorce?*

Bobby: *I just need space.*

And space included every girl in the city, and then about 50% of the girls in neighboring cities. I ran into him often—at bars, at shows, at places I used to love before they became a minefield of 'some random' in his lap. Every time I saw him, I felt like a ghost in my own life.

The worst part was that I still wanted him to notice me.

We lost touch.

I wish I could say I got over him quickly. That I wiped my hands clean of the mess he left behind and moved the hell on.

I didn't. I became different. Not crying-on-the-bathroom-floor-while-Kelly-Clarkson-belts-'Since You've Been Gone' level of depressed. But I was moodier. Darker. A version of myself I didn't recognize.

My heart wasn't just broken, it was wrecked.

So I went home. Not to my apartment and not to my friends, but to the one place that had always offered peace in the middle of chaos.

I went home to my mom. I stayed with her for a few days, curled up in my childhood bed, seeking comfort in the one person I knew wouldn't leave me.

I laid in her lap and cried. And cried. And cried.

Until I had nothing left—no more tears. And yeah, maybe our time together was short-lived, but I'd never felt this kind of pain before. Because I'd never been on this side of it. I'd only ever had one boyfriend before Bobby. Craig. And I was the one who ended it. I broke his heart.

This was karma.

I thought my heart was rock solid. I thought I was unbreakable.

Then came Bobby. And now, I wasn't sure if I would ever be whole again.

***

The first year after Bobby was a slow detox.

At first, I measured time in Bobby units. One week since I last saw him. One month since we last talked. Three months since I finally stopped expecting his name to pop up on my phone.

The ache dulled, but it never really left. There were still moments: a song, a scent, a stupid inside joke that no one else would get. But I was moving on. I dated. Nothing serious. No one that made my pulse race. But I was trying.

And then, before I knew it, a whole year had passed.

Bobby was a ghost I had finally learned to live with.

———

The universe is a cruel bitch. I had gone two full years without running into him or hearing his voice. Two full years without Bobby Fucking Radio DJ Dickweed messing with my head. I had healed. I was dating a great guy named Brian.

And then, one night, there he was. I didn't see him at first. Didn't feel the shift in the air or sense the cosmic joke unfolding in real time. I was just at the bar with my friends, drinking my usual Captain and Coke, when Georgia stiffened next to me.

"Sam," she said, gripping my arm.

I turned. And there he was.

Same black hoodie. Same stupid faux hawk. My stomach flipped. Not in the way it used to. Not with excitement. With something closer to annoyance. Because how dare he still look like that? Like no time had passed? Like he could just exist in the same space as me without a warning label?

I sucked in a breath, turning back to Georgia.

"Let's get another drink."

"Good call."

And so we exited stage left. Luckily, he hadn't seen us sneak away, or so I thought. How I'd managed to avoid him for this long was impressive. But I wasn't about to fuck that streak up now.

I was happy and with someone else. I didn't need Bobby fucking with my progress. So we made our way to the other end of the bar, ordered a Captain and Coke, and ignored him. For an hour, I ignored him.

At one point, Georgia headed to the restroom to freshen her make-up. And there I was sitting alone on the bar deck. I should've gone with her.

I felt it before I saw him. That prickling at the back of my neck, the kind that tells you you're being watched.

I turned, and there he was, Bobby, already walking toward me. I should've run and pretended I didn't see him. I should've done anything but sit there and let him get closer. But part of me wanted to talk to him, because are you really ever over the person who broke your heart?

I don't think so. I think, no matter how much time passes, they'll always own a piece of it. And maybe, I wanted to see if he still owned mine.

At first, it was idle chit chat.

"Hey," he said.

"Hey," I replied.

"How have you been?" he asked.

"Good, you?" I responded.

And then, he dropped the bomb.

"I'm sorry," Bobby said.

I blinked. "For?"

"For making the biggest mistake of my life," he said.

Here we go.

"For letting your slip away."

Jesus Christ.

"I can't stop thinking about us and what we could've been."

Oh, fuck off.

"You're the girl I want next to me when I fall asleep at night."

This is embarrassing.

"You're the girl I want to make eggs for every Sunday," Bobby professed. "I just... I think I love you."

And that's when my brain short-circuited. I stared intently at him. Listened to his full admission. It was everything I'd ever wanted to hear from him. I would've sold an organ on the black market to hear these words.

And yet, the only thing that came to my mind at that moment was that *I don't even like eggs.*

So I just continued to listen.

And waited for the moment when he realized...

He was two years too late.

Alec: Toxic Hottie

"I Write Sins Not Tragedies – Panic! At The Disco"

It had been about a year since Bobby stomped on my heart like he was Michael Flatley, mid–Riverdance, performing an encore on my shattered dignity.

Georgia had been trying to convince me to "broaden my horizons"—her words, not mine—and dip my toes back into the dating pool. But frankly, I wasn't even sure I remembered how to swim. I felt like a shell of a human.

She'd signed up for a local speed dating event and was determined to drag me along.

Um, hard pass.

But, I figured I could at least glance at the questionnaire they made participants fill out.

Speed Dating Questionnaire. *Oh, this should be good.*

"List 10 facts about yourself to help us place you with your best match."

Only ten?

Are these supposed to be *fun* facts? *Weird* facts? Is there a scoring system? Is there a man in a back room grading me on compatibility? Is there a specificity to the fact compilation that I need to consider, sir?

Whatever. Here's Sam in a nutshell:

1. I don't kill things. I just don't. I like animals more than people. I don't kill ants. I don't kill spiders. *Not all spiders are biters, okay?* It is our responsibility to look after one another, big, small, spider, raccoon. Does it really matter?

2. I consider myself a foodie, but not in a 'let me tell you about my dry-aged Wagyu while I swirl my wine and judge your palate' kind of way. I just love a good meal. Hot dog cart in NYC. Michelin-star restaurant in LA. Doesn't matter. If it's good, I'm there.

3. I have an irrational fear of dark water. I joke that I'm afraid of clowns, chainsaws, and centipedes—and I am—but if you offered me a million dollars to stand face-to-face with any of them, I'd ask you where to sign. If you offered me the same amount to jump into the ocean or an open body of dark water, I'd tell you to kick rocks.

4. I pace when I talk on the phone. I don't know why, I just do. If I'm on a call, I will walk in circles around my house, pacing to the rhythm of the conversation.

5. Silence is my happy place. As an adult, I crave alone time. No music. No TV. No background noise. Just absolute silence. I need to recharge in complete solitude.

6. I've been interrupted my entire life, so I've turned into a fast talker. People are always waiting for their turn to speak instead of actually listening, so I started talking at lightning speed to get my entire thought out before I was inevitably cut off. Now, when I'm overly excited or heartbroken, really any extreme emotion, I talk so fast that even Busta Rhymes would tell me to slow the hell down.

7. I take two showers a day. Minimum. One in the morning to start fresh, one at night to wash the day away. If I work out? That's a third. If I feel vaguely sweaty for any reason? Make it four. Basically, I spend half my life in water that isn't terrifyingly dark.

8. If I don't know you, I thrive in awkward silences. Watching people squirm? 10 out of 10. Absolutely makes my day. But if you're one of my people, forget it. I will prioritize your feelings over mine *every single time* and be miserable so you can be happy.

9. I swear to God, I'm psychic. I know it sounds ridiculous, but my gut has *never, ever* let me down. It's scary. But in the best possible way.

10. I startle easily. If you so much as enter a room too
    quietly while I'm focused on something, I *will* jump
    like I've just been shot. I am 100% convinced I have
    shaved years off my life due to the sheer number of
    unnecessary jump scares I've endured from unsuspect-
    ing coworkers, family members, and my own goddamn
    reflection.

I've been described as quirky.

According to the Oxford Dictionary, quirky is an adjective used
to characterize someone by peculiar or unexpected traits.

Peculiar. Unexpected. Unique. One of a kind.

I'll *fucking* take it.

———ele———

Speed dating questionnaire: completed. Emotional baggage:
still fully packed.

Because no matter how many boxes I checked or witty facts I
listed, one thing remained painfully true—I wasn't over Bobby.
Not even close. It had been a year!!!

Definitely, not a proud moment.

Heartbreak had a funny way of sticking to your skin, refusing to let
you move on, even when you swore you were ready. And because

the universe loves a cruel joke, Bobby and I had suddenly started bumping into each other everywhere.

Before, we had worked at the same radio station but barely crossed paths. Now it was like I had been thrown into a teeny-bop musical on repeat, except instead of choreographed dance numbers and a happy ending, I was stuck watching my ex move on in real-time.

Every event, every venue, every goddamn show, he was there. I couldn't escape him. And it was wreaking havoc on my brain, my heart, and my body. This part-time gig was starting to lose its appeal, and I wasn't sure the freebies were worth it anymore.

So when Warped Tour rolled around, I told myself I was fine. That I was going to enjoy the music, work my shift at the promotions table, and not think about Bobby. Easier said than done on this hot summer day.

It was mid-afternoon, the sun relentless, beating down on the festival grounds as bands screamed into microphones and punk rockers moved like waves across the crowd.

I was at the promotions booth, half-distracted, counting down the minutes until my shift ended, when I felt eyes on me. I glanced up. And that's when I saw him. Blond hair, blue eyes, a jawline that looked like it had been carved by the gods themselves. He was, without a doubt, one of the hottest guys I'd seen in a long time.

He was walking toward me, and I immediately straightened, pretending like I wasn't just zoning out seconds before. He picked up a free T-shirt, flipping it between his hands, and then he looked at me and locked in. It wasn't just a glance, it was a moment. A flicker of recognition between two people who had never met but somehow already knew what was coming next.

Then came the smile. Dear god, that smile. The kind of slow, dangerous, dimpled grin that could make you agree to just about anything before you even knew what you were agreeing to.

"You work here?" he asked, voice smooth, casual, as he pulled a sticker from the pile on the table.

"For now," I said, matching his energy. "But in exactly ten minutes, I'm off-duty and free to make terrible decisions."

His grin widened. "I like terrible decisions."

My stomach did a full-blown stage dive. But before I could respond, ask his name, or figure out what the hell just happened, he tucked the sticker in his pocket and disappeared into the crowd.

I blinked. And just like that, he was gone.

I shook my head, exhaling sharply. Warped Tour was chaos. People came, people went. Maybe I'd never see him again and that would be that.

Once my shift ended, I wandered to one of the main stages, the air thick with sweat-spilled beer, and the unmistakable electricity of live music. Rise Against filled the speakers, their lyrics threading through the crowd like a heartbeat, and I let it rush through me, reminding me why I loved this scene, why I loved being here, getting lost in something bigger than myself.

Then, through the mass of people, I saw him. Blond hair, sun-kissed and messy, and that ridiculously perfect smile. He was with his friends, all of them completely in their own world, jumping, singing along, losing themselves in the music. And then, like it was the easiest thing in the world, he found me again.

Our eyes met. Three seconds passed. This time, he didn't disappear. Instead, he started walking straight toward me.

The crowd swelled and moved around us, but Alec was locked in, zero hesitation, and no distractions. His confidence was casual, effortless, like he already knew how this was going to play out.

By the time he reached me, I could feel the warmth radiating off his skin, and he smelled like a mix of something clean with a hint of sex wax.

"You again," he said, smirking as he tipped his chin toward me.

I arched an eyebrow. "You again."

He tucked his hands into his pockets, rocking back slightly on his heels. "You come to Warped often?"

I smirked. "You use that line often?"

He laughed, and I saw his shirt stretch across his muscular chest.

"Yup," he admitted, tilting his head. "What's your name?"

It took me a second to answer, not because I was hesitating, but because for once, I wasn't thinking about Bobby.

"Sam," I finally said.

"Alec," he introduced himself.

We were still standing in the middle of the crowd, bodies brushing past us, music vibrating through our feet, but it was like the world had shrunk down to just us.

His friends called for him. They were headed to another stage. He hesitated for a moment and then, without breaking eye contact, he held out his hand.

"Your phone," he said.

I blinked. "My phone?"

"Your phone," he repeated, still smiling.

I didn't move right away. After a beat, I dug my phone out of my back pocket and placed it in his waiting hand. He unlocked the screen without hesitation, added his number, and then sent himself a text from my phone.

"There," he said, handing it back.

I stared down at the message thread that now existed between us.

Alec: *Don't be a stranger.*

I glanced up, unable to fight my grin.

"That's your move?" I teased.

He shrugged. "It worked, didn't it?"

Before I could respond, his friends called his name one last time from across the crowd. He turned his head slightly, then back to me. Blonde. Blue eyes. A smile that could get me to do things I had no business doing. I needed to be careful with this one.

"When are you gonna text me, Sam?"

I smirked, tucking my phone back into my pocket.

"When your phone rings."

He grinned. And then, just like before, he disappeared into the sea of people.

But this time, I knew I'd see him again.

—ele—

Alec made me laugh, not just a chuckle, or a polite, amused reaction, but real, belly-hurting, tear-inducing laughter. And after everything I had been through with Bobby, laughter was something I hadn't even realized I needed.

We'd only been hanging out for a couple of weeks, but I liked him. Not in an obsessive, doodle-his-name-in-hearts-on-my-notebook kind of way, but still, I liked him.

We were sitting on the couch in my apartment, legs tangled comfortably, my laptop open between us as he introduced me to Dane Cook.

"You're seriously telling me you've never watched his stand-up?" he asked, feigning offense as he scrolled through videos.

I shrugged, popping a piece of popcorn into my mouth. "I've heard of him. Never really paid attention, though."

Alec's jaw dropped like I had just insulted his entire existence.

"Okay. Nope. That ends now," he declared, clicking on a video. "Prepare to have your life changed forever."

And, honestly, it kind of was.

Because ten minutes in, I was crying from laughter, gripping my stomach as Alec quoted along with the skit like he had memorized it years ago. We went down a rabbit hole of stand-up specials, one after another, staying up way too late, laughing until I physically couldn't breathe.

Alec was easy. Easy on the eyes, easy to be around, easy to forget that life was complicated and messy and full of things that hurt. With him, everything felt lighter.

And I liked that. I liked him.

―――ℓℓℓ――――

"Aren't we supposed to be going out tonight?" Georgia asked, leaning against my bedroom door frame, arms crossed.

I barely looked up from my phone, reading Alec's text.

"Change of plans. He wants to hang out."

Georgia let out a slow exhale, tapping her fingers against the wall.

"So you're bailing on me again?" she asked, her voice careful, measured.

"That's a hair dramatic," I said, rolling my eyes.

I stood up and grabbed my bag. "We'll go out another night," I smiled.

She studied me for a second before shaking her head. *"Yup."*

I ignored the way her tone pricked at something in my chest as I slipped past her and out the door.

―――ℓℓℓ――――

The next weekend, I was dog-sitting for my boss while she was away on vacation, which meant I had free rein of her massive house, complete with a pool and a ridiculous outdoor sound system. So, naturally, I invited Alec over.

It started innocently enough with a few drinks, while the dogs ran in circles around us and we lounged by the pool, soaking in the humid summer night. Then, at some point, Alec looked at me, grinning that dangerous grin of his.

"You're not gonna get in?" he asked, his voice all teasing, all challenge.

I tilted my head, arching a brow. "I don't know. Maybe I just like watching you suffer in this heat."

Alec grinned, standing up and pulling his shirt over his head in one swift motion. And Jesus, he was built. Golden skin, abs cut like they belonged in a magazine, shoulders broad and strong. I was staring, and I didn't even care enough to be subtle about it.

Before I could come up with some kind of snarky comeback, Alec walked straight to the edge of the pool and dove in headfirst.

I let out a laugh as he surfaced, running his fingers through his soaking blond hair, water cascading down his face, his chest, disappearing beneath the dark water. He shook his head, sending droplets flying everywhere. Then, with a wicked grin, he reached out and splashed me. I shrieked, jumping back, my hands flying up in protest.

"You gonna come do something about it," he taunted.

I huffed, rolling my eyes, before standing up and peeling my tank top over my head.

Alec stilled.

His eyes dragged over me, dark and hooded as I shimmied out of my shorts, standing there in just my bra and underwear. The heat between us shifted, playfulness morphing into something heavier.

I held his gaze as I walked to the pool's edge, dipped my toe into the water, and then walked over to the steps and slowly descended into the pool. Teasing him with every step.

I slipped beneath the surface, the cool water rushing over my skin, swallowing the heat of the evening. When I emerged, Alec was already there waiting—his eyes locked onto mine, dark and unreadable.

And then, we collided. His hands found my hips beneath the water, pulling me into him, my legs floating up, tangling around his waist. For a second, neither of us spoke. The only sound was the soft rippling of water, the distant hum of music playing from the outdoor speakers, and the sound of our breathing. Then, slowly, Alec reached up, fingers brushing along my jaw, my cheekbone, my bottom lip.

"You're trouble," he murmured.

I smirked, my heart hammering against my ribs. "You just figuring that out now?"

He let out a low chuckle, and then he kissed me. And holy hell.

It was slow at first. A lazy kind of kiss, like he was taking his time, savoring, teasing. But then my arms wrapped around his neck, my nails digging in slightly, my body pressing closer, and that was all the invitation he needed. The kiss deepened, his lips demanding attention.

The water moved around us, his arms strong and steady, pushing me to the edge of the pool. I pressed against him, his fingers exploring, teasing, tracing every inch of bare skin they could find.

I felt weightless, completely lost in him, in the heat of his mouth, in the way his hands moved over my back, my ribs, my hips. His lips moved down my jaw, my neck, the slope of my shoulder, sending electricity sparking along my skin.

I exhaled slowly, my fingers slipping into his damp hair.

He smirked against my skin, his voice husky, wrecked.

"You feel good."

I didn't answer. I just pulled him back to me, my lips crashing into his again, my entire body singing from the heat of it.

The night was nothing short of scandalous.

Some memories fade. This one never did.

It was one of those perfect weekends. The kind you don't realize is going to matter forever until it's already behind you.

Alec and I took a trip to a local beach town, one of those sleepy little spots where the waves stretched for miles and the world seemed to slow down. It wasn't far, just about an hour and a half awaybut something about getting in his 4Runner, rolling the windows down, and blasting Dane Cook skits like they were our personal road trip playlist made it feel like we were driving into another world.

We camped in tents at a local campsite, laughing as we struggled to set up the poles, pretending like we knew what we were doing. The whole trip was thrown together on a whim, but somehow, those were always the best kinds.

That night, we ate greasy, oversized pizza, sitting on the boardwalk with our feet dangling over the sand, and the ocean humming behind us. The sky was a deep, inky blue, and the stars scattered like someone had spilled glitter across it.

The sounds of the ocean were different at night. During the day, it was loud, constant, demanding. But now it was calmer with a steady rhythm that matched the rise and fall of my breath.

It was the time of year when the days were hot but the nights were cool and brisk. The air inside the tent was warm, filled with salt and something electric. The kind of heat that wasn't stifling, but charged, buzzing just beneath the surface.

We lay on top of a blanket, the distant crash of waves filling the silence. Alec was beside me, stretched out on his back, one arm tucked behind his head, the other reaching toward me, tracing small, absentminded patterns along the inside of my wrist.

For a while, we just lay there, listening to the waves crash against the shore, letting the silence stretch between us.

Then, in the dark, his fingers laced through mine. It was such a simple thing. But it felt like the beginning of something. I turned onto my side, resting my head against my arm, memorizing his face, his delicious cologne, the way this moment felt. He looked over at me, his eyes searching.

"This is kinda perfect," he murmured, fingers tracing lazy circles against my arm.

For once, nothing was pulling me back into reality. No thoughts about what came next, no lingering doubts, no weight pressing against my chest.

Just him. Just this.

I turned my head to look at him, my pulse slow and steady. "You're kinda perfect."

"Come here," he whispered.

He leaned over, brushing his lips against mine, soft at first, barely there, like a question. I didn't hesitate. I answered by pulling him closer.

The kiss deepened, slow and unhurried, like we had all the time in the world. He skimmed his fingers over my skin. They were warm against the cool night air, his touch deliberate and intoxicating. His hands were gentle but firm, exploring and learning. Like every touch was a silent question and my body was the answer.

Everywhere he touched, I felt alive. I shifted closer, my body molding against his, the heat between us suddenly unbearable. The world outside the tent didn't exist anymore. No other people. No thoughts of yesterday, no worries about tomorrow. The rustling of fabric, the warmth of his skin against mine, the way he whispered my name between kisses like it was something sacred. It wasn't rushed or careless. It was us, moving together under a sky full of stars, wrapped in nothing but each other and the sounds of the ocean outside.

And when it was over, when we were breathless and tangled in the blanket, his fingers traced lazy circles along my shoulder.

I closed my eyes, listening to the waves, to the steady rhythm of his breathing, to the way the world felt soft and slow and infinite. And for the first time in a long time, I didn't feel like I was chasing something. I just felt present. Whole.

This wasn't our first time and it wouldn't be our last. But it was certainly one of the most intimate moments I've ever had with someone.

That night was nothing short of magic.

———

Until it wasn't.

At some point in the middle of the night, the nightmare came for me.

I shot upright in the tent, screaming. Not the kind of startled gasp where you blink a few times and go back to sleep. No. This was full-blown horror-movie screaming.

For a split second, I had no idea where I was. Everything was dark. My heart was pounding and I couldn't seem to pull air into my lungs.

"Sam. Hey. Hey."

Alec's hands were on my shoulders, steady but gentle, grounding me back in reality.

"You're okay," he said softly.

I blinked, trying to orient myself. The sound of the ocean slowly replaced the chaos in my head. The tent. The beach. Alec.

Right. Outer Banks. Not whatever twisted psychological thriller my brain had decided to produce tonight.

I exhaled slowly.

"Fuck," I muttered, dragging a hand down my face.

Alec let out a quiet laugh.

Unfortunately, this wasn't a new occurrence, and it wasn't the first time Alec had to calm me down after a night terror.

I've always had nightmares. Not the kind where you wake up a little startled, roll over, and go back to sleep. No. Mine were cinematic horror flicks directed by my subconscious, complete with disturbing plot twists, vivid imagery, and enough psychological torment to give Freud an aneurysm.

And they weren't a passing phase.

When I was a kid, the routine was always the same: I'd jolt awake drenched in sweat, convinced some shadowy figure was lurking in the corner. My tiny feet would hit the floor as I sprinted to my parents' room, desperate for comfort.

And my parents, well, let's just say, they were not about that life.

"No, Sam," my mom would mumble from the pillow. "Go back to bed."

If my dad was even home, he'd grunt something similar.

So naturally, I'd resort to Plan B. My sister. I'd sneak into her room, curl up at the foot of her bed like a traumatized golden retriever, and pray she wouldn't notice. But you guessed it. She always noticed, and when she did, it was game over.

"Get. Out."

And before I could plead my case, I'd be physically kicked out. Not metaphorically. A literal foot-to-body punt straight to the floor.

Plan C was full-on survival mode.

I'd crawl into my closet, wrap myself in a blanket like some haunted burrito, and sit there rocking back and forth until the sun came up. This went on for years.

In college, it didn't get any better. My suite mate nearly had a heart attack the first time she heard me scream bloody murder at 3 a.m., bursting into my room like she was about to thwart an active crime scene.

My roommates hated me. There's nothing like waking up to a blood-curdling scream to really set the tone for a terrible night's sleep.

In my adult years, oh, my poor boyfriends. Every single one of them, at some point, had the horror-movie experience of lying next to me, peacefully sleeping, only to be jolted awake by me sitting straight up in bed, mid-scream like I'd just been possessed by a demon.

Nothing says "sexy girlfriend" like someone who wakes up like they're auditioning for *The Exorcist*.

Fun fact—that's not so fun. I have hypnopompic hallucinations and sleep paralysis. NBD, I hit the jackpot.

Honestly, at this point, I just accept it. Some people collect porcelain dolls. Some people have irrational fears of escalators. Me, I have recurring night terrors.

Alec brushed a strand of hair off my face bringing me back to reality.

"You okay?"

I nodded. "Yeah. Sorry I ruined the whole magical beach-camping vibe."

"I thought we were reliving a scene from *Friday the 13th*. So the fact that Jason Voorhees isn't outside our tent is music to my ears," Alec smirked.

Mortified, I laid my head on his chest and nuzzled into him. His scent filling my nose and calming my still pounding heart.

Night terror: 1. Sam's dignity: 0.

<hr>

The next morning, we piled into Alec's dust-covered 4Runner, the sun already climbing high in the sky as he steered us onto the sand.

Driving on the beach felt like we were breaking the rules, like we weren't supposed to be there, even though we were. The tires sank into the soft earth beneath us, leaving a trail of uneven tracks as the salty air rushed through the open windows.

We were on a mission—to find the wild horses. The Outer Banks were famous for them, the way they roamed free along the dunes, untamed and beautiful.

Except, apparently, they were really good at hiding, because after an hour of driving, scanning every inch of grass-covered hills and open stretches of sand, we still hadn't found a single one.

I sighed dramatically, leaning back against the seat. "Maybe they're just an urban legend."

Alec chuckled, tapping his fingers against the steering wheel. "Oh, they exist. They're just making us work for it."

Another twenty minutes passed and nothing.

I turned to him, narrowing my eyes. "Okay, admit it. You have no idea where you're going."

He smirked. "Not a clue."

I groaned, throwing my head back against the seat. And then Alec braked suddenly, kicking up a spray of sand. My body jolted forward, but before I could complain, he pointed. And there they were. A small herd of wild horses, standing at the crest of a dune, their dark manes rippling in the wind, completely untouched by the world around them. They were majestic, surreal, like something out of a dream.

My phone buzzed.

I glanced at the screen. Nana calling.

I silenced it with a tap. "I'll call her later," I whispered to no one.

Alec didn't ask who it was. He just kept staring at the wild horses, mesmerized.

I never did call her back.

We got out of his vehicle, ensuring a safe distance, and embraced the moment and the beauty of the horse ahead.

I stared, entranced, momentarily forgetting how to breathe. Alec was right behind me, wrapping his arms around me and pulling me into his chest. His chin rested lightly on my shoulder, his breath warm against my skin. And just like that, we watched them together.

There were no words, no sounds, just the wind, the waves, us, and the horses. A moment that felt like it was meant to last forever.

There was something about that trip, about the way everything felt so effortless, so weightless, so perfectly ours.

The drive back was just as easy as the drive there. More Dane Cook, more laughter, more of him making stupid jokes at me from the driver's seat, trying to get me to spit out my drink.

And maybe that was what made it one of my favorite memories of any boyfriend I ever had. Because it wasn't about the big, grand moments. It was about the little ones. The inside jokes, the stupid skits, the way he always pulled me closer when he thought I was getting cold. The way he looked at me like he knew we were in the middle of something we'd never be able to recreate.

And he was right. Because I've had a lot of nights, a lot of road trips, and a lot of people who came and went.

But that night. That trip. Well, that one stayed.

—ele—

But perfection isn't attainable. And no matter how magical the fairytale might seem, reality has a tendency of slapping you square in the face and waking you from whatever dream state you're in.

I should have seen it coming. Alec was twenty-four and still living with his parents.

"You want to move out and get your own place?" I asked him.

"Why would I want to do that?" was his only response.

That alone should have made me pause, not because it was a dealbreaker, but because of what it meant. That he wasn't trying to build something on his own. That he was comfortable exactly where he was. A lack of ambition. A lack of commitment.

But I ignored it. Because he was beautiful, and made me laugh. Because when he kissed me, the whole world fell away. And because, only days ago, we had spent one of the most magical nights of my life together.

I thought we were on the same page. That all changed one sunny day on our way to see a movie.

I pulled into the driveway of Alec's parents' house, rolling to a stop, half-distracted as I reached for my phone. I had only been waiting there for a couple of minutes when I figured, *why not just go knock?*

Alec answered, and immediately, I knew something was off.

His jaw tightened, his grip on the doorknob white-knuckled as he stepped onto the porch like he was blocking the entrance. His eyes flicked behind him for a second, toward the house, toward whatever he didn't want me to see, before snapping back to me.

His voice was low, clipped. "You should've just waited in the car."

I blinked. "What?"

He exhaled sharply, running a hand through his already messy blond hair.

"My parents are inside," he said like that explained everything. Like I had committed some major offense just by existing too close to his front door.

I was just picking him up for a movie. It was a casual night with a casual greeting. A completely normal thing to do.

I frowned. "Okay? I wasn't planning on asking them for your hand in marriage, Alec. I was just saying hi."

He didn't smile or soften. He didn't brush it off like the ridiculous overreaction that it was. Instead, he looked at me like I'd crossed some invisible line. And suddenly, the warmth from our weekend in the OBX felt like a distant memory. I wasn't worthy of stepping inside his house. I wasn't worthy of meeting his parents, even in passing.

A breath of silence stretched between us, heavy, awkward. And then his mother appeared in the doorway.

"Alec, who's this?" She asked, her voice warm and welcoming.

I barely had time to react before she opened the door wider, smiling from ear to ear.

"No one," he quickly responded.

His mother and I just stared at one another. My cheeks flushed with embarrassment.

"I mean, my friend, Sam," he said, trying to recover.

Talk about a punch to the fucking gut.

I searched his face, trying to find the same guy who had held me under the stars, who had wrapped his arms around me while we had watched wild horses, who had made me feel like magic was real. But he wasn't there. Not anymore. Not in this moment. Instead, he was this. This strange, rigid version of himself that made me feel like I was nothing more than an inconvenience.

His mother, clearly trying to break the tension, continued, "Why don't you come on in, Sam? I was just about to make some tea."

Alec stiffened beside me. His jaw clenched, his entire body tensing like his mother had just invited me into a top-secret government facility instead of their perfectly normal, middle-class home.

For a split second, I hesitated. I could feel Alec's eyes on me, his silent protest, his unspoken plea for me to turn around, get back in the car, and pretend this didn't happen. But I didn't. Because his mother was already holding the door open, already looking at me like she genuinely wanted me there. So I smiled, stepping past Alec and into the house. I could practically hear his frustrated sigh behind me.

The inside of Alec's house was bright, inviting, and homey. It smelled like laundry and something sweet, like banana bread or cinnamon rolls. A framed picture of Alec's high school graduation sat on the mantle, right next to what looked like a family vacation photo from years ago. This wasn't some mysterious, off-limits place. It was just a home.

Alec's dad was sitting at the kitchen counter, working on a crossword puzzle, but as soon as I walked in, he put his pencil down and smiled in my direction.

"Well hello, I'm Rick," he said, introducing himself. He stood and shook my hand.

"It's always nice to meet Alec's friends. Especially when they're as pretty as you."

I raised an eyebrow, glancing at Alec, who was standing stiffly near the door, clearly regretting every decision that led to this moment.

I laughed softly, uncomfortably, and then thanked him. "I'm Sam. Nice to meet you."

Alec glared at his parents like he had just been betrayed. His mom, trying her best to eliminate the palpable strain in the room, asked, "I just put on a pot of tea. Do you have time to stay for a cup before you two head out?"

Before I could say anything, Alec cut in.

"She doesn't," he said quickly, his tone borderline sharp.

His mom frowned. "Oh. Well, maybe next time, then."

Alec didn't answer. Instead, he turned to me, jerking his head toward the door. "We should go."

The shift was so sudden, so stark, that for a second, I just stared at him. I had just spent five minutes in his house, and his parents were nothing but kind, open, and welcoming. So why was he acting like this was the worst thing that had ever happened to him?

I gave his parents a small smile. "It was really nice to meet you both."

"You too, sweetheart," his mother responded, squeezing my hand.

I turned to follow Alec, who was already halfway out the door, his entire body radiating irritation.

The second we stepped outside before I could even say a word, he rounded on me.

"I told you to wait in the car," he muttered under his breath, pulling the door shut behind him.

I blinked, caught between confusion and something dangerously close to anger. "I wasn't breaking into your house, Alec. I knocked on the door. That's what normal people do."

His jaw ticked. "I just didn't want to make a thing out of this," he said, motioning his hands back and forth between me and him.

I let out a sharp laugh, crossing my arms. "Make a thing out of what? I said hello to your parents. Get a grip."

He sighed, running a hand over his face like I was the problem here. Like I had done something wrong just by existing in the same space as his family.

And suddenly, the warmth of the weekend in the OBX felt miles away.

I should have been upset. I should have called him out, demanded to know why he was making something out of nothing. But instead, I just shook my head, walked back to my car, and got in.

He followed, sliding into the passenger seat, and I started the engine without another word. Suddenly, the magic we had built, didn't feel so real anymore.

Red flags don't always come waving, bright and obvious, demanding your attention. Sometimes, they come quietly. They come in the form of a missed call that never gets returned. A promise made that's conveniently forgotten. A gut feeling that you ignore because you want to believe in the version of him you built in your head.

But hindsight is a real bitch.

—ele—

My lease was up on my one-bedroom apartment and I needed help moving. Nothing crazy, just a few heavy boxes, a couple of pieces of furniture, a few hours of effort. The kind of thing a boyfriend wouldn't think twice about helping with.

But Alec wasn't my boyfriend. He'd made that abundantly clear at his parent's house. However, I needed some help and Alec said he'd be there. He agreed to help.

So I waited and waited. And then I realized I was waiting for nothing because Alec never showed. No text, no call, and no responses to any of my calls or texts either. Nothing.

I tried to convince myself that maybe he got caught up at work, maybe he forgot, maybe there was a reason.

But the truth was, he wasn't a good guy. Because a good guy doesn't make promises just to break them. A good guy doesn't let you move an entire damn apartment by yourself while he's off doing something—anything—other than keeping his word.

I should have seen it then. I should have known.

But that was the thing about red flags. They were so easy to ignore when you still wanted the story to have a happy ending.

Because, God, he was so damn hot.

———ele———

Alec was a bartender at one of the busiest spots on the oceanfront. It was one of those places where the music was too loud, the drinks were overpriced, and the bartenders were treated like local celebrities. Alec thrived in that environment. The never-ending attention. It was his scene.

Sometimes I'd stop by when he was working. The second I walked into the bar, he'd light up, flashing that million-dollar smile like I'd just made his whole night. I'd sit at the bar with my friends, and he'd move behind the counter like he owned the place. There were nights he even let me choose the music that blared through the sound system behind the bar.

This particular night was humid, the kind of thick summer heat that clung to your skin, and made everything feel heavier, stickier, and more electric. Inside, the bar was packed, the air buzzing with music, laughter, the clinking of glasses.

Alec flashed that smile to every girl who leaned over the counter, whispering orders in a way that made them giggle. Alec, flirting. Because that's what he did. Because "a guy with a girlfriend doesn't make as much money as a guy who's single and available," he'd tell me.

I didn't mind it. Not at first, anyway. I told myself it was part of the job. But I hated watching his hands brush against someone else's as he slid them their drink. I hated the way they leaned in, batting their lashes like they had a shot. But above all, I hated the way he never shut it down.

Because, frankly, I think he got off on it. On the attention and the game. Hell, on me watching, knowing I was stewing, knowing that no matter how much it pissed me off, I wasn't going anywhere.

And maybe that was the worst part. Because as much as it burned me up inside, it turned me on too.

I rolled my eyes as another girl leaned over the bar, her cleavage practically resting on the counter, twirling her straw like she actually had a chance with him. She was just another faceless, plain Jane, vying for his attention. She thought she had a shot? Pathetic.

On this particular night, I barely made it through the crowd before I felt his hand curl around my wrist, pulling me toward the back hallway. Through the dimly lit corridor, past the swinging kitchen doors, until we were pushing through the employee exit, stepping into the warm night air.

The second the door shut behind us, my back was against the brick wall. His hands found my hips, pressing me into the rough surface, his body close enough to make my breath catch.

"I hate it when you flirt with other girls," I murmured, my voice lower than I intended, thick with something I didn't want to name.

Alec grinned, tilting his head, smug and knowing.

"How much do you hate it?" he asked, his lips brushing over my jaw, kissing his way down my neck, slow and lazy, like he had all the time in the world.

I shivered, fingers curling into the fabric of his shirt, hating that he had this effect on me. He was playing with fire, and he knew it. Because he liked me like this. He liked me jealous, desperate, and falling right into the palm of his hand. And who knows, I'm pretty sure I liked it too.

So I stopped fighting it. I yanked him closer, and let my lips crash into his. The kiss wasn't soft. It was needy, consuming, and frantic. I was desperate to erase the taste of all the girls he'd been charming inside. His hands tightened on my waist, fingers digging into my skin as he pressed me harder against the brick, deepening the kiss until I forgot everything but the heat of his mouth on mine.

He groaned against my lips and pulled away. He looked at me, smirked, and walked back into the bar. The door shutting behind him.

I was completely and utterly wrecked by him. I wanted him. NO. I needed him and he knew it. Hell, I think he enjoyed knowing it.

It was a game to him. The flirting, the teasing, the way he kept me on edge, always craving more.

But then, one night, the rules changed.

The bar was buzzing with the usual low hum of conversations and clinking glasses, the air thick with cheap cologne. I walked in, my heels clicking against the worn floorboards, and I spotted him almost immediately behind the bar.

I smiled, instinctively, expecting the usual, his eyes catching mine, the barely-there smirk, the quiet acknowledgment that, despite everything, I was still his favorite game to play.

But this time, he didn't even acknowledge me. Before I could even say hello, he was turning away, deliberately, like I wasn't even there. Like I was just another face in the crowd and he didn't even know me. Not just like he didn't see me, but like I was a stranger. Like I was any other girl walking into his bar.

And something about that moment hit me harder than it should have.

Because suddenly I was sixteen again, standing in the middle of a gymnasium during a pep rally, scanning the bleachers for somewhere—anywhere—to sit.

I remember walking up and down the rows, pretending I was looking for someone specific, when in reality I was just hoping someone would wave me over.

No one did.

That was the first time I understood what it meant to feel invisible. The emptiness rising in my chest as I looked for anyone to sit with. The tight knot in my stomach twisted, a sickening realization settling in that I was truly on my own. And then came the sharp, undeniable awareness of what it meant to be alone.

Not alone in the sense of standing by yourself. Alone in the sense that no one was saving you a seat. No one was scanning the crowd hoping to find your face.

Because when you're a kid, your imagination fills the gaps. But eventually you grow up, and the rules change. Friendships matter. Connection matters. But most of all, being chosen matters.

And when you realize you're not worth someone's time or attention—that kind of loneliness doesn't just sit in your chest, it guts you.

Standing in that bar, watching Alec laugh with a group of women like I didn't exist, I felt that same sick, hollow drop in my stomach. Like I had just walked into a room where there was no seat for me.

I watched as he leaned in close when they ordered, flashing that same dimpled, devastating smile he used on me like they were the only ones in the room.

And I saw the way his tips piled up. That should've been reason enough to flip him the bird on my way out the door. But instead, I made excuses for him. Convincing myself it wasn't that bad, that I was overreacting, that this was just how he was.

It didn't dawn on me that I was just something he could have when he wanted, ignore when he didn't, and drop completely when it no longer suited him. And it took me far too long to figure that out.

Because, truthfully, he was the hottest guy I'd ever dated.

And I was too blinded by my own vapid, shitty personality to see past it.

~~ee~~

I met him at a chain restaurant that smelled like haunted memories of your childhood. Dirty mop water and the lingering scent of overly fried food.

The second I walked in, I felt it. Something was off.

Alec was already at the table when I arrived, his hands folded in front of him, his shoulders squared like he was preparing for battle.

I sat down, we placed our orders, and before we even got our food—before I had even taken a sip of my damn drink—he was breaking up with me. No lead-in. No build-up. Just a casual, gut-punch of a statement.

I did the only thing I could think to do. I got up and walked straight out the door. No words. No reaction. Because if I didn't walk away right then, I was either going to cry or scream. And I refused to give him the satisfaction of either.

I made it to the parking lot before I stopped, gripping the edge of a concrete barrier, sucking in a deep breath, and forcing the lump in my throat back down where it belonged.

I wouldn't let him make me feel small. I wouldn't let him think he had this much power over me.

So, I straightened my shoulders, turned around, and walked back inside. Back to the table. And back to him. Fucking. Smirking.

The most vivid thing I remember about that night wasn't even Alec's excuse. It wasn't his bullshit, half-hearted explanation. It was the waiter. Poor guy. He knew exactly what was happening—could see it all over my face. He approached slowly, shifting awkwardly, trying to time his interruptions just right.

"Uh, so," he cleared his throat, holding the tray in front of him like a shield, "I've got your drinks."

Alec barely acknowledged him, nodding stiffly. I, however, wanted desperately for this man to interrupt. To make this moment go away. Please, drop a plate. Start a grease fire. Fake a heart attack. Something.

But no. Instead, he just delicately placed my water in front of me like he was offering last rites, then scampered away as fast as he came.

I wanted to cry. I wanted to flip the damn table. Instead, I sat there. Seething.

Alec's reasoning was bullshit. Something about not wanting a serious relationship, something about feeling pressure, something about him being a little bitch.

I barely remembered leaving the restaurant. One second, I was sitting across from Alec, staring at him in complete disbelief as he ended things like we were nothing.

The next, I was in my car, gripping the steering wheel so hard my knuckles ached. My breathing was uneven, my pulse hammering, but I refused to cry.

Not over him and not tonight.

I exhaled sharply, leaning my head back against the seat, staring at the roof of my car like it might hold some kind of answer.

I felt hollow. Not because I loved him. Not because I wanted him back. But because I had let him do this to me. Because I had wasted so much of myself on a guy who could sit across from me in a shitty chain restaurant, order his drink, and break up with me before the food even arrived—like I was nothing.

And actually, fucking smirk at me. He acted like I hadn't given him my time, my body, my love. Like I hadn't let him wreck me in a million small, sharp ways.

I clenched my jaw, my throat tight. I could text Georgia. I could go home, put on a sad movie, let myself feel this, and process it like a mature human being.

But I didn't want to be mature. I wanted to burn it all to the fucking ground.

I reached for my phone, my hands steady now, my mind clearer than it had been in months. I wasn't crying or spiraling. I was done.

Alec had always been able to get away with treating me like an afterthought. Like I'd always be there, waiting for him, ready to forgive and forget. But tonight, I was rewriting the script.

I scrolled through my contacts, my pulse quickening. I didn't hesitate for even a second. I clicked his best friend's name and typed out a message.

Me: *Hey, what are you up to tonight?*

I hit send. I threw my phone onto the passenger seat, put my car in drive, and didn't look back.

And then, I did what any hot, pissed-off woman in her twenties would do. That same night, I went and fucked his best friend.

And I don't regret it one bit.

———

The restaurant was busier than usual, but it was Sunday brunch, and we locals dubbed that special day of the week "Sunday Funday."

I was sitting at a booth with Georgia, picking at the half-eaten bennie on my plate, barely hearing whatever story she was telling me. Because my mind was somewhere else. Somewhere blonde. Somewhere named Alec.

It had been weeks since the breakup. Weeks since I'd last seen him, last touched him, last let him get under my skin. And yet, here I was, still thinking about him.

Georgia, however, hadn't thought about him once. Because Georgia had already decided exactly who Alec was, and she hated him. Watching me spiral through the highs and lows of his flippant bullshit didn't sit well with her. She was protective, of course, because I was her best friend.

"You know," she said, stirring her drink with her straw, her tone entirely too casual. "I really thought the biggest idiot you'd ever date was going to be Bobby."

I shot her a look. "Here we go."

She shrugged. "But no. Turns out, you had more surprises in store. Because Alec is an insufferable prick."

I sighed, taking a sip of my drink. "Well, that took a turn."

"Watching you date him was like watching a really bad reality show where the girl refuses to see the red flags because the guy has abs," she said, exasperated.

I rolled my eyes.

"But those abs were really, really nice," I muttered.

Georgia let out a sharp, humorless laugh.

"Yeah, well, he was an asshole," she countered. "He treated you like an accessory. Like a pair of designer sunglasses, he could take off whenever they didn't match his outfit."

I scowled. "Here we go again with the theatrics."

"Am I?" she challenged, narrowing her eyes. "Because last time I checked, your boyfriend pretending not to know you in public is a pretty big fucking deal."

I opened my mouth to fire back, to defend him but was interrupted by a girl at the table parallel to us.

"Excuse me, I don't mean to interrupt, but I just have to tell you how pretty you are!" she said, beaming.

I just stared at her blankly and took a sip of my drink, Georgia's words still ringing in my head.

Her smile faltered for a second before she nodded, turning back to her friend.

Georgia, beside me, gave me a shocked look. "Jesus, Sam!"

I rolled my eyes. "What?"

She sighed, shaking her head.

"Nothing. Just miss my best friend not acting like an asshole."

I froze. Only for a second. But long enough to feel the sting. I had nothing because she was right. And I hated that she was right.

Georgia took a sip of her drink, changing the subject. "Look, I'm just saying, you could do a hell of a lot better than Alec."

I scoffed. "Yea, Like who?"

Georgia grinned, slow and wicked.

"Oh, I don't know. Maybe his best friend."

I choked on my drink. "That was a one-time, poorly executed, horribly-timed lapse in judgment that we will never, ever speak of again."

She just smirked, raising her glass in a mock toast.

"Something to think about," she said, before taking a sip.

And for the first time that day, I laughed. However, her words still stung, even though she wasn't wrong.

She sighed, tilting her head. "You weren't you when you were with him. And I think some part of you knows that."

I swallowed, my throat tight.

"You deserve better," she added, squeezing my hand briefly before reaching for her drink.

And maybe she was right. Maybe I did.

—ell—

Falling for Alec wasn't just about loving him. It was about becoming someone else entirely. I didn't notice it at first. How could I? I was too busy getting lost in the fantasy of us. Too busy chasing the high, believing in the illusion, and convincing myself that what we had was special. That he was special.

But slowly—bit by bit, piece by piece—I stopped recognizing myself.

And the worst part was that I didn't even care. I started to mirror him. The way he carried himself, cocky, untouchable, like he was above it all. The way he treated people, like they were background characters in his movie like they existed to serve his ego. And the more time I spent with him, the more that version of me grew.

The asshole version.

The version that rolled her eyes at people who didn't matter and acted like she was better than everyone in the room. Or the version that laughed at the wrong jokes, picked up the wrong habits, and lost pieces of herself in the process.

And I lost people. Friends who had been there before Alec, friends who saw me slipping and tried to pull me back. But I didn't listen. Because I didn't want to hear it.

Loving Alec came with a price. And that price was me.

Because by the time I finally opened my eyes, by the time I finally saw the wreckage I had left behind, I realized I had nothing left of myself.

I didn't want to accept that I had changed, that I had become cold, detached, and someone I wasn't proud to be. Because deep down, I knew it was true. And admitting it meant I had to face what I had become.

I had let him turn me into a person I didn't even like. And that was the hardest thing to forgive.

But that didn't stop my pulse from skipping when Alec's name showed up on my phone a week later.

$$\sim\!\!\ell\ell\!\!\sim$$

He texted me one night out of the blue. No warning or preamble. Just a message that made my stomach flip in the worst, most unfair way.

Alec: *You up?*

I should have ignored it. I should have listened to the little voice in my head screaming *NO.*

But nostalgia is a dangerous thing. Because instead of telling him to go to hell, instead of reminding myself why I had walked away in the first place, I was slipping into the passenger seat of his 4Runner, seatbelt clicking into place like muscle memory.

And just like that, I was right back where I started. Right back to us and to the way it used to be. To laughing, smiling, kissing, and believing—for just one second—that maybe I hadn't imagined the Alec I once loved.

The road stretched ahead of us, dark and endless, the only sound was the steady hum of the tires against the pavement and the distant whisper of music from the speakers.

I glanced at him out of the corner of my eye. He looked the same. Sharp jawline, sun-streaked blond hair, and that intoxicating smile that could unravel me in seconds.

But something was different. Or maybe I was different. Still, I let myself sink into the moment.

We talked about life, work, the usual bullshit. We talked about new bands, the albums they had just released, which ones were good, which ones were trash.

And when he laughed—really laughed, the kind that reached his eyes—I felt something shift in my chest. Something I didn't want to feel. Something that made me ache for the Alec from the Outer Banks trip. The Alec who made me feel safe and held me under the stars. The Alec who hadn't yet ruined me.

Before I knew it, the 4Runner had drifted off the main road, the tires crunching over sand as we pulled onto the beach. He cut the engine, turned to me, and for a second, we just sat there.

The ocean stretched out in front of us, dark and infinite, the waves rolling in with a rhythmic crash, the night sky above clear and endless.

Alec leaned his head back against the seat, exhaling slowly before looking at me with that smile. The one that had always been my undoing.

"Come with me," he said.

Then, without waiting for my answer, he reached into the backseat, grabbed a blanket, and pushed open his door. And like a fool, I followed.

We laid the blanket down just far enough from the waves, the cool breeze tugging at our clothes, carrying the scent of salt and memories. I stretched out beside him, staring up at the sky, the stars winking down like they knew something I didn't.

For the first time in a long time, it didn't feel tense, or like we were standing on the wreckage of what we used to be. It just felt like us. Like we had never fallen apart.

We talked about everything and nothing. Mainly stupid inside jokes that still made us laugh. And for a few fleeting hours, I let myself forget the past. Forget the pain, the mistakes, the red flags.

Forget the way he had shut me out, pushed me away, made me feel like nothing.

Because here, under the stars, on this beach that felt like it belonged to only us, none of that existed.

Then he turned his head toward me, his gaze soft, unreadable. And I knew what was coming before it even happened.

He reached out, his fingers tracing the inside of my wrist, a touch so familiar it sent a shiver through me. Then, slowly and deliberately, he leaned in. When his lips met mine, slow, soft, and familiar, I let him.

Because at that moment, it wasn't about the past or the pain he caused. It wasn't about the inevitable disaster waiting for me on the other side of this decision. It was about this feeling and illusion. It was a dangerous and addictive lie we both wanted to believe.

Because for the first time in a long time, it wasn't messy. It wasn't toxic.

It was just Alec and Sam. Love and respect. It was just us.

And against every warning in my head, every red flag I had ignored, every instinct screaming that I was walking straight back into the fire—I let it happen. And, of course, we'd break up again, because that was inevitable.

Again and again. A vicious cycle.

A story we kept rewriting, even though we already knew the ending.

A love story that was never really love at all.

Lee: Reckless Abandon

"More than a Feeling – Boston"

I 'm not necessarily proud of the person I was in my early twenties. I was rude, inconsiderate, and entirely self-involved. After Bobby and Alec, I was struggling to remember the person I used to be. The one who had integrity and stood up for what was right. Instead, I'd become someone who took what she wanted, regardless of who was in the way.

I surrounded myself with people just as thoughtless as I was. Maybe it was to disguise what I'd become. Maybe I just didn't care.

And that's how I met Lee.

Lee wasn't just another guy. He was a player's player, the kind of man whose name came with a warning label. A mutual friend introduced us, begrudgingly, as she also had a thing for him. I should've felt bad about how hard I pursued him. I didn't. I reiterate I wasn't proud of myself.

The first time I saw him was at a movie theater. I'd gone with some mutual friends, and even though Alec was there, we were on the outs. The only reason I agreed to go was to throw a punch his way—emotional, of course—and show him exactly what he was missing.

My jeans were too tight, my graphic tee read *"You were never my boyfriend"* (subtlety had never been my strong suit), and I was bored and bitter enough to let my gaze wander the second we got inside.

That's when I saw him. Lee was standing in line at the concession stand, all 6'1 of him, perfectly sculpted, leaning on one arm like he owned the room. We locked eyes, no, collided. It was instant. Kismet. The kind of connection that made my skin buzz from my nose to my toes.

And I knew, right then, that I was going to eat this man alive. Bit by delicious bit.

When we got ushered into the theater, I made sure we ended up next to each other. A silent agreement. Our arms brushed when we sat down, and I swear I heard him exhale like he felt it too. But neither of us spoke. Not yet.

We didn't exchange numbers that night. Didn't need to. Because when I got home, I did what any shamelessly determined woman with a Wi-Fi connection would do—I found him on social.

His profile was a goldmine of information. Firefighter. Long family legacy. Loved the same obscure bands I did (a rarity). And a lifeguard on the weekends. Which meant one glorious thing: a metric ton of shirtless photos.

Don't mind if I do.

I went to sleep that night fully satisfied with my research. When I woke up, my inbox greeted me with a friend request from Lee. That didn't take long.

I smirked, stretching like a cat across my bed before I hit accept. The game was on.

His message came first. Predictable.

Lee: *So, are you the kind of girl who internet stalks, or did we just both happen to be mildly obsessed with each other?*

I grinned.

Me: *So you admit, you're mildly obsessed with me?*
Lee: *You didn't answer my question.*
Me: *I don't stalk. I research. Big difference.*
Lee: *Oh? And what did your "research" tell you about me?*
Me: *That you're a bit unhinged, choosing to run into burning build-ings for a profession.*
Lee: *Aren't we all a bit unhinged?*

Isn't that the goddamn truth.

Lee: *What else?*
Me: *That you're allergic to shirts.*
Lee: *Ah, so you lingered a bit too long in the photo section? Me too.*
Me: *Guessing you liked what you saw?*

I was shamelessly flirting. The bravado, the seduction. I was laying it on thick.

Lee: *We can both admit we had similar reactions in the photo sections.*
Me: Maybe
Lee: *So where does this leave us?*
Me: *As undiagnosed attention-seekers. If I had to guess, I'd say there's a 75% chance that you're a Leo. 90% chance of thinking you can out-flirt me.*
Lee: *Wrong. Pisces. 100% chance I can out-flirt you.*
Me: *Bold claim for a man who still hasn't asked me out.*
Lee: *Is that a challenge?*
Me: *It's a fact. But now I'm curious—are you scared?*

I barely had time to toss my phone aside before it buzzed again.

Lee: *Friday. 8 pm. Wear something I'll want to peel off.*

Oh, this was going to be fun.

I flopped back onto my bed, cocky as hell. A fling is exactly what I needed to win Alec back.
And Lee was about to be eating out of the palm of my hand.

The sound of an engine rumbling outside my window made me pause mid-touchup, my mascara wand hovering in the air.

It wasn't just any engine. It was the kind that growled, a deep, throaty rev that sent vibrations through the pavement before the headlights even hit the glass.

I stepped closer to the window and pulled the curtain back just enough to see him. Lee was climbing out of his lifted F-250, and I swear I felt my pulse skip as he swung the door shut with one fluid motion. The truck itself was a statement. The kind of thing that made girls weak in the knees before they even saw who was behind the wheel.

And there he was. Dark jeans that hugged his ridiculously perfect ass. A blue t-shirt stretched just enough across his chest and arms to make my mouth go dry. He ran a hand over his head, shifting his weight, completely at ease, like he had no idea the effect he had on people. Or worse. Like he knew exactly what he was doing.

I grinned, taking one last glance in the mirror before heading downstairs.

Time to play.

⁓ℓℓ⁓

Our first date was at the Norva, a gritty little concert venue where indie bands came to bleed their hearts out.

From Autumn to Ashes blared through the speakers, the drums rattling the floor beneath us, and I was in my element.

Bodies moved ahead of us in the pit, the crowd swelling and pulsing with the music, but my focus stayed locked on Lee. The neon glow from the bar lights cast sharp shadows across his jawline, his blue eyes watching me like he was already playing the endgame in his head.

I took a slow sip from my drink, deliberately letting my lips linger around the straw before pulling it away. He noticed. Of course, he noticed.

"You're full of surprises," he said, leaning in just enough that I could feel the heat of him against my bare shoulder.

I arched an eyebrow, feigning innocence. "How so?"

He smirked, tilting his head toward the stage. "Girls don't usually listen to screamo music."

I let that hang in the air for a second before I turned, locking my gaze with his.

"I like to hear people scream."

His expression flickered, just for a second. A slow inhale, a shift of his stance, like he was recalculating the game we were playing.

And then, just to drive it home, I took the straw between my lips, keeping eye contact as I sipped, dragging it slowly before setting the drink down.

Lee exhaled, "We'll see about that."

I smiled. I was intoxicating and I knew it.

The night had settled around us, the chaos of the concert still thrumming through our veins as we stood outside my apartment.

Lee had one hand braced against his truck, fingers flexing slightly like he was holding himself back. The other was tucked casually in his pocket, but I could feel the tension radiating off of him. It was the kind that crackled in the space between us, waiting for someone to make the first move.

I wasn't in the habit of waiting.

"You keep looking at me like that," I murmured, stepping closer, "and I'm going to have to take a big bite."

His lips curved into that infuriating smile, the kind that sent a slow roll of heat down my spine.

A challenge.

I met his gaze and tilted my head just slightly, my confidence unwavering.

"Guess there's only one way to find out," he responded, eyes flicking to my lips just once before he moved.

And when he kissed me, it was like he'd already mapped out every inch of my mouth in his head.

There was no hesitation, just pure, practiced control. His lips were firm, and deliberate, molding against mine like he knew exactly how to unravel me. One hand slid up my back, fingers pressing into my side, pulling me flush against him while the other tangled into my hair at the base of my neck, holding me there, owning the moment completely.

I exhaled a soft gasp against his mouth, and he took it as permission, deepening the kiss, teasing, tasting. His tongue traced the seam of my lips, slow and devastatingly confident like he had all the time in the world and wasn't about to rush through something this good.

I didn't even realize my hands had found his shirt until I felt the heat of his skin beneath my fingertips, the fabric pulled tight across his chest. His body was solid, his muscles taut beneath my touch, and he felt just as good as he looked.

His fingers tightened in my hair, and the slight pull sent a shiver down my spine, making my knees threaten to give out.

Jesus Christ.

He kissed like he did everything else—with certainty. With a knowledge that he knew exactly how to take his time, exactly how to keep someone wanting more. This man knew exactly what to do. Period.

I was breathless when he finally pulled back, just enough that I could feel his breath ghosting against my lips.

He tilted his head slightly, studying me like he was memorizing the effect he had. And then he smiled one last time.

"Knew you'd taste good," he murmured.

I exhaled a laugh, still lightheaded, still reeling. "You kiss like you've been waiting to do that all night."

His grip on my waist tightened just a fraction. "That's because I have."

I bit my lip, already craving more.

Lee's dark gaze flicked to my mouth one last time before he finally stepped back, hands still lingering at my waist like he wasn't quite ready to let go.

"Goodnight, Sam," he said, voice rough.

I barely had time to respond before he turned, walked back to his truck, and left me standing there with my heart hammering, my lips still tingling, and my mind completely wrecked. *I am still in control. Samantha, lock this shit down.*

But, I recognized quickly that this wasn't just a kiss.

This was the start of something dangerous.

—✐—

It took two weeks for Lee to seal the deal. Two weeks of late-night conversations, of teasing touches that lingered but never crossed the line, of him kissing me like he wanted more, but then pulling away just when it got dangerous. Two weeks of restraint that completely threw me off my game.

For someone with a reputation like his, this wasn't what I expected. At all.

I had gone into this knowing exactly who he was. A player and a heartbreaker. A guy who probably had a rotation of women blowing up his phone at any given moment. I wasn't delusional. I knew what I was signing up for.

Besides, this wasn't about Lee. This was about Alec. Lee was supposed to be a ploy, a distraction. Something to wave in Alec's face to make him see exactly what he lost. And at first, that's all he was.

But two weeks?

Maybe, the rumors weren't true and Lee wasn't the smooth-talking womanizer I had been warned about. Maybe he was just a really good guy.

The patience, the way he looked at me like he was seeing something deeper like he wasn't just here for the chase, it was messing with me.

And after that explosive kiss? What was I to think?

Or maybe, I thought as I stared at the text telling me to come over, he was just really, really good at playing the game.

—— *ell* ——

I barely knocked anymore. Lee had a habit of leaving the garage door unlocked, so I'd slip in, past the rows of firefighter gear and neatly stacked weights, straight into the kitchen like I belonged there. Because at this point, I kind of did.

Nights had blurred together—movie after movie, curled up on his couch, my legs draped over his lap, the TV flickering across his skin. He never missed a chance to touch me, his fingers lazily tapping my thigh, his palm spreading warm against my knee.

My phone buzzed. Nana was calling again, probably with another update on her neighbor's gallbladder surgery.

I rolled my eyes. "Her timing is impeccable," I muttered, hitting decline.

I'd call her later. But that was a worry for future me. Right now, back to Lee.

We were becoming comfortable, too comfortable. I didn't want Lee to be comfortable. I wanted reckless, exciting, fleeting. I wanted passion with an expiration date. Alec. *Eye on the prize, Sam.*

Lee, though? Lee was playing the longest game I'd ever seen. He never rushed. Never pushed. He'd tangle his fingers in my hair, kiss me breathless, press me up against the counter, the couch, the door and then, nothing.

If it weren't for those makeout sessions that left me dizzy, gripping onto him like he was the only thing keeping me upright, I would've thought he had friend-zoned me. Which, honestly, would've been completely counterproductive to my mission. Because I showed up to his house like a model out of a damn Victoria's Secret catalog. Leggings that hugged my ass just right, tiny crop tops that left little to the imagination, off-the-shoulder sweaters that slid down in just the right way when I reached for the remote. Effortless seduction.

And yet, nothing. Only suggestive comments, and obvious stares, but no attempt to push things further.

The most I got was that damn smirk of his, that knowing look he'd give me right before pulling me into his lap, kissing me like he was starving, only to pull away before things could go too far.

It was infuriating.

And, if I was being honest, it was working. Because by the time he finally told me to come over that night, I knew. I knew I wasn't walking into his house to watch another movie. I wasn't showing up in another cute outfit just to see if he'd break first.

Hell or high water, I was going to make him beg for it by the end of the night.

My fingers hovered over the door handle, heart pounding in my chest. I had done this before. I wasn't nervous. But this was different. This was Lee. And everything about Lee was intense.

I took a slow breath, pushed the door open, and stepped inside.

Lee's house was dimly lit, the glow from a single lamp casting long shadows along the walls. The air smelled like faint cologne and something recognizable, something unmistakably male. My skin prickled, my body already reacting to a presence I hadn't even seen yet.

Then I saw him.

Lee leaned against the kitchen counter, beer in hand, his dark eyes slowly dragging over me, taking in every inch like he was memorizing me before even touching me.

"You look," he murmured, barely able to finish his sentence.

I smirked, closing the space between us. "This old thing."

I knew exactly what I was doing. The outfit hugged every curve, leaving absolutely nothing to the imagination. The skirt hem barely extended past my most indecent regions.

He set his beer down and reached for me, one fluid movement, all certainty and intent. His hands found my hips, fingers pressing just enough to make me aware of them.

"Too bad you'll be out of it soon," he said, voice low and dangerous.

And then he kissed me. Devoured me.

It wasn't slow, wasn't testing the waters like before. It was heat, urgency, an inevitability finally tipping over the edge. His lips owned mine, his hands seizing me like he wasn't about to let go. And I didn't want him to.

Somehow, we ended up in his bedroom. I wasn't entirely sure how we got there, only that my back met the mattress, and his body followed.

I felt every single bit of him against me and he felt good. Rock hard, throbbing, and ready.

I exhaled a sensual laugh, dragging my nails down the front of his denim. "So much for the theory that guys with big trucks are compensating for something."

His lips trailed down my neck, pausing at my collarbone. Nipping.

"Guess you'll have to find out for yourself."

Well. Don't mind if I do.

Lee was absolutely not overcompensating. And boy did he prove it that night. Twice.

Lee wasn't just good. He was ruin-me-for-anyone-else, knock-the-breath-out-of-me, make-me-forget-my-own-name good. Every touch was intoxicating, every movement precise, like he already knew exactly what I needed before I even did.

The way his hips pressed perfectly into my core, the rhythmic beat was a masterful performance. He didn't rush. He took his time, making a slow, delicious game of it. He teased me and I begged for more before he finally gave me exactly what I wanted.

He nipped, and licked, and sucked. Every inch of my body. One final nibble and I was absolutely, unequivocally wrecked.

At some point, my hands found his shoulders, my head tilting back as a shattered gasp escaped my lips.

Lee grinned against my skin, murmuring against my ear, "You like hearing people scream, right?"

"Me too," he finished. Both figuratively, and literally.

I let out a breathless, completely exhausted laugh.

Jesus.

This man was going to kill me.

I pulled into the lot, my tires crunching over gravel as I eased into an open space outside the firehouse. The sun was just starting to set, the air thick with heat and smoke from whatever training burn they had done earlier.

I didn't text Lee that I was coming, I didn't have to. He had mentioned earlier that they were between calls, so I figured I'd take my chances and surprise him. Not that showing up unannounced was anything new.

As I stepped out of my car, tugging at the hem of my too-short-for-this-place skirt, I could feel eyes on me. I'd developed a habit of wearing skirts whenever I was around Lee. Made for easier access.

A low whistle cut through the humid air.

"Jesus, Lee, you didn't tell us you had a supermodel stopping by today."

I turned toward the voice, catching sight of three of his colleagues standing by the bay doors, leaning against the engine, all of them looking at me like I had just walked onto the set of a calendar shoot.

"Shit," one of them muttered. "If I knew we got visitors like this, I would've signed up for overtime."

A ripple of laughter followed, and I smirked, totally unbothered.

Lee's voice cut through them like a whip.

"Y'all are gonna get your asses kicked if you keep talking."

"Oh, is lil Lee gonna come smack me?" one of the guys quipped.

Lee chuckled. "Not by me. By her."

That's a good boy.

I turned just as he stepped out from behind one of the rigs, his turnout pants slung low over his hips, suspenders hanging loose over a sweat-dampened navy t-shirt. My stomach flipped.

I had seen Lee in a hundred different settings—in bars, in bed, in the dim glow of a movie theater. But this was different. Something about the grit of the firehouse, the way his shirt clung to him, the way his crew immediately shut the hell up when he spoke, it did something to me. And judging by the way his dark eyes dragged over me, it was doing something to him too.

I took a slow step forward, tilting my head, pushing the game just a little.

"What, you don't want your friends flirting with me?" I teased, watching as his jaw tightened.

He took two strides toward me, no hesitation, no space left between us.

"They can look," he murmured, voice low enough for only me to hear.

His fingers ghosted along my thigh, a barely-there touch that sent heat licking up my spine.

"But I'm the only one who gets to touch."

I exhaled, my pulse hammering as his hand tightened just enough to make my breath catch and for my center to tremble. Needing his touch.

The others were still watching, pretending to mind their own business, but I could feel their amused glances from a distance.

Lee leaned in, his breath warm against my ear.

"Come with me," he murmured, voice dark and full of something dangerous.

I didn't even hesitate.

<center>~~~</center>

The firehouse was all steel and concrete, but behind the rig, tucked just out of sight, the world shrank down to just us.

The second we were alone, Lee spun me fast, my back pressing against the cool metal of his truck. The contrast of cold steel and his burning heat was lethal. His hands were everywhere, gripping and caressing, like he was seconds from losing every ounce of control he had left.

"That was fun," I breathed, my fingers curling into the front of his t-shirt, dragging him closer.

His lips licked over my jaw, down my neck, and over the tops of my breasts. I pressed against him, ensuring they were peaking out of my too-thin tank top.

"You think I liked watching them drool over you?" His voice was rough, edged with something dangerous and dark.

I smirked. "I think it turned you on."

His hand moved to my inner thigh and his fingers began reaching higher and higher until he was mere inches away from my heated core.

"You have no idea," he growled.

And then, before I could throw another smug remark his way, he kissed me. It was needy and anguished. Claiming.

Then he pressed his fingers into my slick depths reaching for the spot he knew would make me scream. Scream his name. Scream it, so all of his colleagues could hear who I belonged to.

I melted into him, my back pressed against the truck, my hands sliding over sweat-warmed cotton and hard muscle.

His fingers pulsed into my center, caressing and claiming what was his. I opened my legs more angling just how he wanted, deepening the quivering center that yearned to be released. I was breathless, my knees threatening to give out.

A loud clang echoed somewhere in the distance, a reminder that we weren't exactly in the most private of places. He pulled back just enough to meet my eyes, his own dark and full of heat.

"I need you out of here before I do something that gets me fired," he rasped.

I licked my lips, watching the way his gaze followed the movement, his restraint visibly fraying.

He lifted his finger and placed it onto his tongue, licking and sucking while he pulled it out of his mouth.

"Then maybe you should come find me when you're off shift," I murmured.

His smirk was slow, devastating.

"Oh, we'll finish this with you screaming my name at the end"

And the way he said it?

I had no doubt.

⎯⎯ℓℓ⎯⎯

Lee was a drug. An addiction. I wasn't even aware of it at first, how he'd seeped into my system and rewired my thoughts until everything in my life looped back to him. Needing him, and wanting him. Craving him in a way that felt dangerous.

At first, it was just sex. But not just any sex. Lee was, without a doubt, the best I'd ever had. The kind of mind-altering, body-breaking, ruin-me-for-anyone-else kind of sex that kept me in a state of swollen desire, made me forget my own name, made me wake up in the middle of the night reaching for him again because once wasn't enough. It was never enough.

Because once we crossed that line, we didn't stop.

I'd show up at his house for one thing only. It didn't matter what time it was, didn't matter if I'd already seen him that day—the second we were alone, we were on each other. Hands, mouths, skin, tangled sheets.

I'd conveniently skipped panties because it was easier to corrupt and claim my body if there weren't too many layers in the way.

I'd barely get through the door before he'd have me pinned against it, kissing me, caressing me, devouring me like he was starving. Like he was making up for all the times he made me wait.

And I swore, swore, it was just that. Lust. A high I could control.

But then, somewhere between the clothes hitting the floor and the way his mouth felt against my skin, it shifted. Somewhere between the late-night texts that weren't just about sex, between the way he'd pull me closer after, the way he'd press a lazy kiss against my shoulder like he wasn't ready to let go, I stopped being able to tell the difference between wanting him in my bed and wanting him in my life.

It happened so fast. One minute, I was in control –
arms-length, detached, perfectly balanced. And the next, I was
completely undone. I was enamored with him.

And I didn't even realize it until it was too damn late.

Lee and I had been driving around that afternoon, windows
down, music too loud, laughter spilling between us like it belonged there. The kind of day that felt effortless. The kind of
day that made me believe that maybe, I had finally met someone
who understood me.

I told him I needed to stop by my Nana's house to drop something off. She had recently moved here after Pops died, to be
closer to my mother. He shrugged and said he'd come in too.

I hadn't thought much of it. But then we stepped inside, and
Nana was in the kitchen. She was pulling fresh cookies from
the oven, apron tied tight, flour smudged on her cheek, looking
exactly like she belonged on the cover of a damn Hallmark card.

"Oh, well, hello there," she said, wiping her hands on a dish
towel before giving me a knowing look. The kind only grand-
mothers can give. The kind that said, *Who's this handsome boy,
and why haven't I heard about him?*

Lee stepped forward, hand out, charm already at a hundred.

"Hi, I'm Lee," he said, that smooth, confident ease that always worked on people. "You must be Nana."

She took his hand, patting it like she'd already decided she liked him.

"Well, aren't you polite," she said, eyeing him up and down. "And easy on the eyes."

Lee grinned. "That's what I keep telling her."

I rolled my eyes. Of course, she'd fall for him instantly.

"Are you staying for dinner?" she asked.

I opened my mouth to say no, but Lee beat me to it.

"I'd love to."

And just like that, he was in. It didn't take long for Nana to wrap Lee around her finger. She told stories about her youth, about sneaking out of her house to meet boys, about all the trouble she got into long before I ever existed.

Lee hung on every word. He called her ma'am without sounding forced. He complimented her cooking, and she pretended to wave him off while obviously soaking it in. He made her laugh.

At one point, I got up to grab something from the kitchen, and when I came back, they were deep in conversation. Not just small talk or politeness. But real conversation.

She was telling him about her favorite Patsy Cline song, about how she used to dance in the living room with my grandfather before he passed.

And Lee wasn't just listening, he was seeing her and was completely entranced.

I stood there, unseen for a moment, watching them, watching the way he softened around her. The way he looked at her like she was a story he wanted to read over and over again. And for a second, I thought, *maybe this is it.* Maybe this is the person I get to keep. Maybe he stays.

Later that night, as we sat on my Nana's porch swing, the air thick with the smell of summer rain, Lee nudged my shoulder.

"She's incredible," he said.

I smiled, staring out at the yard, the fireflies blinking against the dark.

"Yeah," I whispered. "She is."

He didn't say anything for a while, just let the quiet settle around us.

Then, in a voice softer than I had ever heard from him, he said, "Both my grandparents have passed, so tonight was nice."

I swallowed hard, something pressing deep in my chest.

"Yeah," I said.

Lee nudged me again, pulling me from my thoughts.

"When I'm old and wrinkled, I want someone to talk about me the way she talks about your Pops," he said with a grin.

I smirked. "So, you're saying that you need a girl who likes Patsy Cline?"

"Nah," he said, leaning back, smiling up at the sky. "Just one who likes me enough to still be around by then."

And for the briefest, smallest moment, I thought *maybe that girl could be me.*

The funny thing about dreams. They're an illusion with only one willing participant.

———ee———

Social media makes everything worse. It tells you things you were never meant to know, shows you things you were never meant to see, and then sits back with popcorn while your brain spirals.

If Lee and I didn't hang out one night, I might have just assumed he was busy, that he had work, that he was tired. I could have let it go, moved on, and enjoyed my own night.

But no, thanks to algorithmic betrayal, I was gifted a front-row seat to his evening without the courtesy of an invite.

And by morning, the notifications start rolling in. A tag here. A story post there. And suddenly, I knew exactly where he was, exactly what he was doing. And worse, exactly who he was with.

A picture of him at a party, beer in hand, a girl tucked under his arm like she belonged there. A video of him at a bar, laughing a little too hard, leaning a little too close. A feed post of a girl kissing his cheek.

I wasn't even looking for it. But there it was. Like a knife to the chest, like my stomach had been ripped out, leaving behind a hollow pit of rage and nausea.

Because while I had been at home, replaying the way he felt, the way he kissed me, the way he made me feel like I was the only one, he had been out doing the exact same thing with someone else.

And then, radio silence for days, sometimes weeks.

The worst part, was that there was never a shift in his behavior – no tension, no cold shoulder, no shift in tone—just a sudden drop off the emotional cliff. Which made it all the more jarring when it happened.

The pit in my stomach never went away. It just sat there, heavy and consuming, stretching wider with each hour that passed without a text, without a call, without a single goddamn acknowledgment that I even existed.

I could have walked away. Should have walked away. But then, out of nowhere, my phone would light up.

Lee: *What are you doing?*

And just like that, the withdrawal was over. It didn't matter that I had spent the last week hating him, swearing I was done, vowing I would never do this again. Didn't matter that I had spent hours scrolling, spiraling, torturing myself over pictures that shattered me. Didn't matter that I had promised myself I was stronger than this.

Because the second I saw his name, I was hooked again. I craved the fix, the drug, the high. The way he made me feel alive. I needed him.

And I hated myself for it.

— ell —

The concert had just ended, the final chords still vibrating in my chest, the air thick with sweat, beer, and that electric post-show buzz. People were filing out, bumping shoulders, laughing too loud, still riding the high.

Lee had his arm slung casually around my waist, the other hand handing me a beer like it was muscle memory, like we'd always been this easy. I took it, grinning up at him, the kind of grin that said *I'm good. This is good.*

And that's when I saw Georgia. She was dating one of the bouncers and had become a regular fixture at this place. She wove through the crowd with that calm, grounded presence of hers, all quiet knowing, and zero bullshit. She smiled when she saw me, pulling me into a hug.

"You look so happy with him," she said, leaning back to study my face, her eyes sharp but gentle.

My stomach dropped. Happy. Was I?

I felt so many emotions in that moment, elated and crushed, all at once. Because Georgia saw what I wanted her to see. What everyone saw. I had never told her the truth. I had never admitted that Lee had the upper hand, and we both knew it. That he called the shots. That at any moment, he could disappear again, just like he always did.

And if Georgia even had the slightest clue that I was this deep, that I was this weak for him, she'd drag me out of this mess kicking and screaming.

So I smiled, let out a small laugh and tucked the truth away where she couldn't find it.

And then, like clockwork, Lee disappeared again.

But when you run in the same friend group, there's no such thing as truly avoiding someone. No clean breaks or pretending they don't exist. Because no matter how hard you try, you will see them again. And tonight, I saw him. Lee had brought a girl, a new one. Someone I'd never seen before. Someone, not me.

She was pretty, of course. They always were. She laughed easily, and touched his arm in that flirty, *I hope you're into me* kind of way. And the worst part is that he let her.

And it hit me like a truck. It wasn't just that he was on a date. It was that he wasn't with me. I had spent so long thinking that no one else could understand him the way I did. That I was different. That despite his disappearances, despite the games, despite the rollercoaster of emotions that left me dizzy and destroyed, I was still the one he wanted.

But tonight, he wasn't looking at me like I was his. So I did the only thing I knew how to do. I threw myself at him. Hard.

I turned up the charm to a hundred, laughed louder, let my hand linger on his shoulder, and let my eyes burn into his, silently daring him to drop the act. To remember who I was. To remember what we were. And for a second, I thought I had him. He looked at me the way he always did like I was a problem he wanted to have.

But then he stepped back.

Stepped. Back.

"I can't," he said, voice low and guarded. "I'm here with her."

I blinked, heat creeping up my neck. I'd been prepared for a lot of things tonight. But not that. Not rejection. And certainly, not him choosing someone else.

I forced out a laugh, pretending like it was no big deal like his words hadn't just cut me open.

"Wow," I scoffed. "So now you're worried about being a dick?"

His jaw tightened, his hands flexing at his sides like he wanted to say something like he wanted to explain. But I didn't wait for an answer. I just turned, grabbed my purse, and then, without thinking, reached for the nearest guy I could toy with to level the playing field. Because if Lee was going to move on in front of me, then so was I.

I desperately tried to ignore the fact that for the first time, maybe ever, Lee was actually being a good guy. But it didn't feel good. It felt like a jab straight to the chest. Because it didn't matter that he was doing the right thing. All I felt in that moment was the rejection. And something shifted. Something inside me cracked open.

A wall started to build, brick by brick, around my heart. And I had no intention of letting him break through it again.

———ℓℓ———

I still remember the call one night that shook me to my core. Not a text—an actual call.

That alone was shocking enough. Lee didn't do calls. Most of our communication existed in the land of delayed replies and half-hearted emojis. But that night, my phone rang, and when I saw his name flash across the screen, I knew something was off.

His voice was strained and raw. He had just come back from a fire call—an accident scene. The victim was a young woman, about my age and build. Unfortunately, she hadn't made it.

His voice cracked when he said it, "I just needed to hear your voice. I needed to know you were okay."

And in that moment, every ghosting, every disappearing act, every breadcrumb of a connection suddenly made sense. He wasn't distant because he didn't care. He was distant because he cared too much and didn't know what to do with it.

There was a goodness in Lee, a softness buried beneath the armor. And maybe that's why I stayed tethered to him, in one form or another. Because even if he wasn't meant to be mine, he still deserved to be loved.

Even if not by me.

When you think you've met the perfect guy and it doesn't work out, the most discouraging thought isn't just the heartbreak, it's the fear that you won't meet anyone like him again. That he was it. That this was your one shot at something great, and you blew it.

Four weeks had passed since I last heard from Lee, and for the first time in months, I was starting to feel like myself again.

Sure, we still bumped into each other now and then, we ran in the same friend group, after all. The most recent run-in was at a group dinner at a Mexican restaurant where I ate my weight in chips and salsa and shamelessly flirted with a newb.

But the good news is that I wasn't walking around in a daze, checking my phone every two minutes, and suffocating in my own silence. I could function at work. I could breathe again. The pit in my stomach had started to shrink, little by little, day by day.

And then my phone buzzed.

It was mid-day, and I was in my office, typing out an email about an upcoming work event. I ignored the vibration at first, assuming it was a friend checking in, the usual "dead or alive?" text. But when I finally glanced at my phone, the name on the screen stopped me cold.

Lee.

My pulse spiked. Fifty conflicting emotions hit me all at once- anger, excitement, skepticism, heartache. I hesitated before opening the message, my hands tightening around the phone like I could physically brace myself for whatever was inside.

Lee: *Do you want to come to my parents' house for Christmas dinner?*

Wait. What?

I stared at the screen, rereading the message over and over again, trying to make sense of it. Did he have the right girl?

We hadn't spoken in almost a month, and now he was inviting me to Christmas dinner with his parents. Maybe it was a mass text or a holiday party. Maybe this wasn't as intimate as it sounded.

I typed back the simplest response I could manage.

Me: *Okay.*

Then I did what any rational person in my position would do. I texted everyone, any mutual friend we had, to see if they had also received the invitation. Not a single one of them had.

Every time Lee ghosted me, it was like another piece of my heart turned to stone. I had built a Great Wall of China-sized defense system around myself, and because of it, I just didn't care as much anymore.

So when he reappeared, like he always did, I felt it less. Little by little, the emotional scale started to tip. And before long, it felt like the ball was bouncing back to my side of the court.

If he called, he called. If I wasn't busy, maybe I'd answer.

And for the first time since I met him, that felt like power.

—ee—

The drums were loud. The band, *ASG*, was in their element, the bass thrumming through my chest, the crowd alive with energy.

Lee stood beside me, a beer in one hand, the other resting on my hip. We were at another concert—our thing, apparently—but for once, I wasn't thinking about us.

Not Lee or the mess of our relationship. Just the music, the moment, the temporary escape. Then my phone vibrated. I felt it in my back pocket, persistent, demanding. I almost ignored it. But when I pulled it out and saw my mother's name on the screen, something shifted. A sinking feeling curled in my stomach. It was past her bedtime, which indicated something wasn't right.

I pushed my way through the sweaty bodies, barely muttering an excuse as I ran for the bathroom, needing somewhere quieter, somewhere I could breathe.

The moment I answered, I knew. Her voice was tight and fragile.

"Nana died about thirty minutes ago."

Everything around me blurred. The noise, the crowd, the electric pulse of the bar, it all faded into the background as my back hit the cold tile wall. Then, slowly, I slid down. I didn't think, didn't speak. I just wrapped my arms around my knees and let the tears fall.

"Sam, you there?" My mother's voice cracked.

I tried to answer, but my lungs felt like they were collapsing in on themselves. I forced myself to breathe, to say something.

"Yes." The word barely scraped past my throat.

"The funeral is Friday. We'll leave for New York tomorrow," she said gently. A pause. Then, softer, "Are you okay?"

Another beat. Another lie.

"Yes."

She hung up and I didn't move.

Nana was really gone. She was my person, my constant. I had spent every summer at her house. I helped her cook for the holidays, sat in waiting rooms with her at doctor's appointments, and told her about every boyfriend.

And yet, in the last six months, I had treated her like she was nothing but a burden.

Maybe because I had become a shit human, a twenty-something prick who cared only about herself. Or maybe it was because I thought I had more time. But I didn't, and now, I would never have time again.

I sat there, unmoving and silent. The tears didn't stop, but I wasn't sobbing. They just kept coming.

I'm sure to any girl who walked in and out of that bathroom, I looked like just another wasted girl on the disgusting floor, too drunk to keep herself upright. But I wasn't drunk. I was just drowning.

I don't know how long I stayed like that, curled up against the tile, my legs stiff, my body numb. Eventually, after what felt like forever, I pushed myself up, wiped the tear tracks from my face, and forced myself back into the bar.

Lee was waiting. He took one look at me and didn't say a word. There was no snarky comment, no joke about bodily functions, no attempt to break the tension. Just silence.

And maybe that was the worst part. Because he knew. He was watching me unravel, watching me hold myself together with shaking hands and a hollow stare, and he knew.

I swallowed hard. My voice came out flat. Emotionless.

"Nana died."

And then I turned around and walked out. I didn't wait for a response. I didn't wait for him to offer me a ride home. Honestly, I didn't care if he called after me.

I just drove, tears burning my vision, fingers gripping the wheel, trying to escape the weight crushing my chest. But there was no escaping this. Because no matter how fast I drove, no matter how hard I tried to outrun the grief, there was one thing I couldn't change.

She was gone.

And so was the part of me that gave a fuck about anyone or anything.

———

The funeral was quiet, too quiet.

People spoke in hushed voices, dabbing at their eyes with tissues, their grief visible, tangible, real.

But me. I didn't cry. I just sat there, hands folded in my lap, staring at nothing, feeling nothing, my mind blank, my body still. A shell of a human.

I remember watching as they lowered Nana's casket into the ground, as people whispered their final goodbyes, as the weight of loss settled over everyone like a suffocating fog.

And still, nothing. Not one tear or a moment of weakness. Just empty.

Afterward, my mother pulled me aside. We stood near the car, away from the clusters of grieving family members, away from the reality I didn't know how to process.

She turned to me, and I could see it, the weight of her own grief pressing down on her, her face drawn tight, eyes red and swollen from crying. But it wasn't just sadness in her expression. It was something else, something I wasn't prepared for. She shook her head, breath shaky, hands trembling at her sides as she looked at me like she didn't recognize me anymore.

And then, her voice breaking, she whispered, "I just lost my mother. And I feel like I'm losing my daughter, too."

The words hit like a slap, but I barely flinched. She let out a shaky, unsteady exhale, pressing the heel of her palm against her chest like she was trying to hold herself together. Like she was trying not to completely fall apart. She looked at me, eyes glassy, full of something devastating.

"You didn't even cry, Sam," she said, her voice cracking. "Not once. Not even for her."

Her breath hitched, and I watched my mother break right in front of me. I should've reached for her, fallen into her arms, let her grief break through my walls. I should've felt something.

But I didn't. Because the truth was, I didn't know how.

I had spent so long building walls, so long convincing myself I didn't need anyone, that by the time I lost the one person who had always been there for me, I didn't know how to grieve. I had forgotten how to feel. I wanted to tell her that. I wanted to tell her that I wasn't okay. That I wasn't heartless, I was just lost.

But instead, I just stood there. Expression blank, voice flat, and said the only thing I was still capable of saying.

"I'm fine."

My mother let out a sharp, broken laugh, one with no humor, just raw, exhausted disbelief.

"You're not fine," she whispered, shaking her head, tears slipping down her face. "You're not fine at all."

And then, she turned and walked away. I stood there, watching her leave, knowing she was right. Knowing that I was so far from fine.

I couldn't even recall what fine felt like.

<center>~~~</center>

After Nana's funeral, after my mother looked at me like I was a stranger, after I felt nothing for far too long, I knew I had to feel something. So when I heard there was a party at Lee's, I went. I was tired of feeling numb.

I wasn't naïve, I knew the kind of parties he threw. Knew there would be a sea of cheap beer, loud music, and bodies draped over each other like they didn't care who was watching.

I walked in, took a deep breath, and let myself pretend this was just another night. That I wasn't still carrying grief like a weight on my back. That I wasn't still haunted by the sound of my mother's voice saying, *I feel like I lost my daughter too.*

I needed to drown it out. Georgia wasn't able to be my plus one so I was flying solo tonight. I grabbed a drink, smiled too easily, and laughed too loud. I let hands that weren't Lee's touch my waist engaging in meaningless conversation to fill the hollow parts of me.

And for a little while, it worked.

The door to his bedroom was locked with him and his ex-girl-friend, Brittany, inside.

Great.

Someone nudged my shoulder, leaned in. "Yeah, he and Brittany disappeared into his room, like, twenty minutes ago." A careless shrug. "Guess they're working things out."

The words barely landed. I stood in the hallway, staring at the door, heart hammering, every beat making my chest tighten, making my fingers curl into fists.

The door was closed. But it didn't have to be open for me to know. For me to feel it. My stomach twisted, my vision blurred, my throat felt like it was closing in on itself.

I wanted to bang on the door, throw it open and scream at him. I wanted to tell him that I loved him, something I probably should've confessed a long time ago. And that despite everything, we should give this a real shot. Because I was tired of feeling numb.

But I didn't. I just stood there. Frozen.

Listening to the muffled sounds from the other side of the door, to the low murmur of his voice, a voice that had once only been for me.

And that was the moment, not when he ghosted me, or when he kissed other girls in bars. This was the moment I let go.

Because suddenly, the numbness I had been living in, it wasn't grief anymore.

It was clarity.

———

Three years had passed. And somehow, Lee and I were still something.

Not lovers, not quite friends, but not nothing, either.

We kept in touch sporadically, meeting up for lunch now and then under the loose pretense of "catching up," but really, it was more about the comfort of familiar chaos. Lee was a good human, flawed, yes, but with a kind of gentle complexity that made him hard to shake. He was one of those people whose sadness wore a disguise. A lost soul dressed in bravado and quick wit. And maybe I saw that part of him because I had pieces of it too.

So when he called and said he didn't have a +1 to the firefighter ball and asked if I'd come with him, I didn't hesitate. There were no expectations or illusions. Just two old friends attending a party.

The firefighter ball felt like something out of a dream. Elegant chandeliers dripped golden light across the ballroom. Laughter and clinking glasses echoed under the hum of low music. Rows of men in uniform stood tall, proud, their dates glowing beside them. The room smelled like cologne, whiskey, and nostalgia. Like the kind of moment you step into and already know you'll never forget.

And Lee treated me like I was his. Like I had never belonged to anyone else and like I wasn't walking into that room wearing someone else's name.

I had told myself it was harmless. That my boyfriend was out of town, that Lee just needed a date, that this was nothing more than a night with a friend.

But the way he looked at me. The way his hand lingered at the small of my back, the way he pulled me closer during slow dances, or how he leaned in when he spoke, his breath warm against my ear—none of it felt harmless.

I let it happen. Let myself sink into the illusion of it all.

One last night. One last moment in time where I could pretend that he had never broken me.

———ℓℓ———

The drive back was quiet. Not awkward, not tense, just thick with something unspoken.

Lee's hands gripped the steering wheel, his jaw tight, his expression unreadable as the streetlights flashed across his face. I kept my hands folded in my lap, my pulse a slow, steady drumbeat in my ears.

He pulled into my driveway and put the truck in park. He didn't move or say a word.

I turned to him, my heart knocking against my ribs as I caught the way his gaze drifted from my lips to my eyes, then back again. And for a second, I thought he was going to kiss me. I felt it in the air, in the space between us that had never really closed, no matter how much time had passed.

But before he could, before he could tilt forward and make me forget who I was supposed to be loyal to, I reached for the door handle and slipped out.

I didn't look back. Didn't wait to see the way his shoulders dropped, the way his fingers flexed on the steering wheel. I just walked inside, closed the door behind me, and leaned against it, my chest rising and falling like I had just run a marathon.

And then, later that night, my phone buzzed. I already knew who it was before I even looked.

Lee: *I thought maybe you'd come back to me.*

A pause.

Lee: *Because I love you.*

I stared at the message, my stomach twisting, my throat closing, my hands gripping the phone so hard my knuckles turned white.

Did I really want to go down this road again with Lee? Even though I knew I loved Lee – part of me always would—I didn't like who I was when I was with him.

Not just because of the way he treated me, but because of the way I let him. Because of the way I chased him when I swore I never would, the way I turned a blind eye to the games and the disappearances, just so I could have him for a little longer.

I'd let myself become reckless, selfish, someone I barely recognized. Someone who gave too much to a person who never gave enough in return. And I couldn't keep self-destructing.

So for the first time in the history of us, I did exactly what he'd always done to me. I didn't text back. I didn't respond.

I disappeared.

Brian: Loverboy

"MakeDamnSure – Taking Back Sunday"

A nother Friday night in December, and there I sat in the quaint Mexican restaurant, shoveling chips, salsa, and white sauce into my mouth like I hadn't eaten in days, waiting impatiently for my food and margaritas to arrive.

I was trying to focus on anything other than Lee, who was conveniently positioned two seats down from me—close enough to feel his presence, far enough to pretend I didn't.

There were about ten of us at the table, but somehow, he'd managed to place himself within earshot. Of course, he had.

Directly across from me sat Leyton, a pleasant yet abrasive fellow with a height disadvantage and an ego to compensate. Maybe 5'5, on a good day. He was known for his booming monologues on topics no one asked about—third-world labor laws, politics, obesity, and the distressing lack of tequila in the aforementioned margaritas.

His temper ran hot when provoked, so I chose the safest survival tactic:

Nod. Smile. Eat chip.

Nod. Smile. Eat chip. Don't think about Lee.

Nod. Smile. Eat chip. Where is my food?

Nod. Smile. Eat chip. My stomach is eating my pancreas.

"Are you always this antsy?"

I blinked. The voice was low, smooth, and entirely unfamiliar.

I turned to find him seated across the table, one over to my right. I hadn't noticed him until now. Dark hair, dark eyes, and a smile that hovered somewhere between charming and trouble.

He was one of Lee's friends and I wasn't in the mood to make any more "new Lee friends" on this particular night.

"Excuse me?" I asked, arching an eyebrow.

He leaned forward slightly, grin widening. "You've shifted in your seat about fifty times in the last five minutes. So, either you're antsy, or you've got an itch you can't quite scratch. If it's the latter, they make creams for that."

I froze mid-chip, glancing toward Lee, who was already smirking like he knew *exactly* where this was going.

"You have me confused with someone who's interested in engaging," I said flatly, dropping the chip back onto my plate. "And, frankly? I'd eat you alive, bird."

"Actual FACT!" Lee barked, raising his beer in agreement.

Oh, fuck right off, Lee.

Don't act like you know me inside and out.

God, I hate that he knows me inside and out.

Lee's friend raised an eyebrow, clearly amused.

Now, I know what you're thinking. Earlier, I mentioned that I had *zero* interest in confrontational banter with Napoleon over there, so why was I welcoming a verbal spar with this unknown guy?

Simple. Leyton tended to escalate quickly, get loud, make a scene, and ruin the night for everyone involved.

This one seemed harmless.

I glanced at him again, lanky but built, broad shoulders, muscles peeking through his RVCA t-shirt, a cocky smirk he hadn't quite earned yet. Maybe it was the boyish grin or the fact that he had a slight slouch, like he was trying to play cool but wasn't fully committed to it. Yeah, I could play with this one.

"Maybe I *want* to be eaten alive," he said smoothly, completely unaware that he had just handed me the match and the lighter.

Lee chuckled and sipped his beer, eyes locked onto mine, already bracing for the fallout.

I don't know if it was Lee's cocky reaction—acting like he knew me better than anyone—or the perfectly timed lull in the restaurant noise that made this next moment feel inevitable. But right then and there, I decided that instead of giving Lee exactly what he expected, me going off on this poor, unfortunate soul, I'd flip the script, and make him eat his words.

I plucked the candied cherry from my untouched strawberry daiquiri. Slowly and deliberately. And then, with zero shame and complete confidence, I twirled it between my lips, sliding it over my tongue, letting my teeth graze the stem before pulling it back. All while still making direct eye contact.

The entire table fell silent. Leyton's jaw dropped. Lee coughed violently, probably regretting every decision he had made that led him to this exact moment.

And Lee's friend? His eyes widened for a split second, and then, slowly, almost defiantly, he grinned ear to ear. At that moment, the entire restaurant ceased to exist.

No more Lee. No more Leyton. No more background noise, no more plates clinking, no more mariachi music over the speakers.

It was just me and—

"I'm Brian," he said, stretching his arm across the table to shake my hand.

"Noted," I replied.

And there it began.

I have this incredibly masochistic trait where I remain friends with most of my ex-boyfriends. It's like some kind of sick personal challenge—how much emotional gymnastics can I perform before I finally give myself a concussion?

So, naturally, every time I hung out with Lee, Brian was in tow, orbiting just close enough to stir something but far enough to remain off-limits.

He had a long-distance girlfriend, which made our bantering feel safe. We could go back and forth, verbal jousts laced with flirtation, daring but not dangerous. Harmless.

I repeat, he had a girlfriend. Then they broke up.

Fair game.

I told myself it didn't change anything and nothing was different. That he was just a friend. A friend who happened to make my pulse quicken when he smiled at me, who had a habit of watching me just a little too long before looking away.

A friend who, at some point, had stopped feeling harmless at all.

⁓ℓℓ⁓

The entire ride home from New York, I stared blankly out the window, my forehead resting against the cool glass. My family and I were driving back from my Nana's funeral. Miles of trees and open highways blurred together, but I barely saw them. My mind was stuck in a loop—my Nana's voice, her laugh, the way she used to hug me so tightly it felt like she could press the sadness out of me. I also couldn't get the argument I'd had with my mother out of my head. She told me that she didn't recognize me anymore. Her disappointment was soul-crushing.

I can't recall how it happened, I had just been hanging out with Lee at an *ASG* concert, but somewhere between the exit signs and the silence, Brian and I started texting.

First, about nothing.

Me: *What's your take on pineapple on pizza?*
Brian: *Hard pass. I have standards. You?*
Me: *If you hate pineapple, we might not be able to continue this conversation.*
Brian: *Wow. This is the hill you want to die on?*

Then, about music.

Me: *Top three bands of all time. No pressure, but your answer determines if we can be friends.*
Brian: *That's an impossible question. I can narrow it down to the Top 30.*

And then, somewhere between a conversation about concerts and an argument over the superior decade of punk rock, I realized I wasn't thinking about the funeral. I wasn't thinking about my Nana's gray-marbled coffin or the moment I saw her face and barely recognized her. I wasn't fighting back tears.

Brian had unknowingly distracted me from drowning. So when he asked, *"You're coming to Lee's party tonight, right?"*

I hesitated. But only for a second.

Me: *Yeah. I'll be there.*

—ℓℓ—

"Are you sure you can't come tonight?" I asked, pressing my phone to my shoulder as I applied mascara.

"No, I'm going on a date with a co-worker," Georgia said, her voice smug.

I narrowed my eyes at my reflection. "Georgia, you do realize once you sleep with him and kick him to the curb, you'll still be forced to see him every single day at work?"

"No I won't," she said breezily. "I'm his manager. I'll just fire him."

I snorted. "Shock me. One day. Just once. Shock me."

She laughed, but my own chuckle felt hollow. The second I hung up the phone, the lump in my throat returned. I closed my eyes, gripping the sink. I needed her tonight. After the week I'd had, the funeral, the grief pressing down on my chest like an anvil, I needed my best friend by my side. I needed her zero fucks attitude to give me strength.

Instead, I was going alone with the ghost of my Nana in my head and the shadow of Lee at the party.

Brian may have extended the invitation, but I had an ulterior motive. I was going to tell Lee how I felt. That somewhere between the pain and the chaos, I still believed in us.

It was reckless and maybe even a little pathetic. But when your world feels like it's unraveling, you reach for the thing that once made you feel alive. And for me, that thing had always been Lee.

I didn't know if seeing Lee would send me over the edge. I didn't know if walking into that party would be the thing that finally broke me.

I'd been here before. That dark place where I was waking up every morning, feeling like a boulder was sitting on my chest. Unable to sleep anymore because I was too exhausted to rest. Not wanting to get out of bed because, frankly, I didn't have the energy.

I'd spent months dragging myself through life like a hollow version of myself. I'd thought, on more than one occasion, that it wouldn't be the worst thing if I got hit by a car. Or if I fell asleep and never woke up.

It was a darkness I knew too well. A version of myself I wasn't proud of. But I also knew how to fight it.

Step one: Find something, anything, to distract me.
Step two: Fake it.

Step three: Put on just enough clothes to not be considered indecent, but enough to leave a man dead in your wake.

Walk into that party alone, but like I owned that shit and my world wasn't already on fire.

———*ele*———

A "Lee party" was a special kind of chaos. On the surface, you never really knew what to expect. But, at the same time, you always knew exactly what to expect. Same old formula, different people, same crowd.

A rotation of underage lifeguard groupies mixed with the skeezy over-20s who were determined to hook up with them. Then there were the regulars, maybe ten of us who had been showing up to these parties long enough to know exactly where the liquor was hidden and which couches had seen too much.

Everyone else was interchangeable.

Lee's stained carpet was proof of past debauchery—beer spills, cheap vodka, and the occasional pizza grease stain. An archaeological site of bad decisions.

I grabbed a Sharpie off the counter and drew an obscenely sexual image on the plywood beer pong table in the kitchen. Upon completing my masterpiece, I decided my second goal would be: Find Lee.

Sure, I'd just been texting back and forth with Brian, and yeah, he seemed cute. But Lee was my drug.

Amidst the crowd of barely legals, I spotted Leyton, tattered baseball cap pulled low, already mid-rant about something I couldn't be bothered to care about.

"Hey," I interrupted. "Have you seen Lee?"

Leyton barely looked up. "Yeah, he's in his room."

The door to Lee's room was shut and locked. My chest twinged like someone had twisted a knife into my heart. I didn't even have to ask, I was very familiar with Lee's playboy ways and what his locked door at a party signified.

"Careful," Brian said, leaning casually against the wall, his boyish, goofy grin firmly in place. "He's got Brittany in there."

Brittany. The ex-girlfriend.

"Ah." Double chest twinge with a side of gut punch. "Good for them," I lied.

He stepped closer, his grin softening into something more serious. His hand brushed my arm, a light touch, like he was testing the waters, and then, Brian closed the space between us in one smooth motion. Before I could process what was happening, his hands found my cheeks, firm but unassuming, and his lips moved to mine.

It wasn't hesitant or awkward. His lips were warm and surprisingly gentle, but the kiss itself was electric, urgent, yet unrushed like he'd been holding it in for weeks.

I was initially caught off guard but my surprise melted into something else entirely as my hands instinctively found his chest, pressing against the heat of him. My pulse quickened as his left hand moved to my waist, his fingers curling just enough around my belt buckle to pull me closer.

Brian was a really good kisser. And this kiss wasn't just good, it was the kind of kiss that ruins you for anyone else. His lips moved against mine with just enough pressure to make me breathless, his fingertips grazing the bare skin between my shirt and jeans. The hallway, the party, Lee—all of it disappeared. There was only Brian, his lips, his hands, the taste of him—spearmint gum mixed with the faintest trace of tequila.

When he pulled back slightly, his breath warm against my cheek, he whispered, "I've wanted to do that for a while now."

He was taller than me, 6'4 to my 5'9, and I was on my tippy toes and yet still not at eye level. I leaned in again, this time pulling him closer, and swirling my fingers through his silky hair. Needless to say, it was the kind of kiss that made you forget the day of the week, your name, or most importantly, who might be watching.

He gently guided me into the adjacent bathroom, the sound of the party fading as the door clicked shut behind us. My back hit the cold tile wall, sending a shiver up my spine, but Brian was there to counter it with the warmth of his touch. His hands trailed from my knee back to my face, his thumbs brushing over my cheekbones as he kissed me again, slower this time, softer but more deliberate.

Sam," he murmured, his breath hot against my cheek as he pulled back slightly. His dark eyes searched mine, and for a split second, I thought he might say something romantic. Instead, his lips quirked into a smile. "You're really bad at pretending you don't like me."

I laughed softly, pulling back just enough to look at him. "And you, my friend, know how to kill a vibe," I teased, running my fingers over his bicep.

His eyes were dark, his expression a mix of amusement and something deeper, something raw. We sank to the cold tile floor, but neither of us seemed to notice. The small, cramped space only made it more intense, and more intimate. Every movement felt amplified, the way his hand skimmed my thigh, or how his lips lingered just a second too long at the corner of my mouth before returning.

We kissed for what felt like hours, breaking apart only to catch our breath, laugh at something ridiculous, or share secrets that felt easier to admit in the haze of the moment. It was intoxicating, and not just the kissing but the way he listened, the way he looked at me like I was the only thing in the world worth paying attention to.

"So why did you and Karlie break up?"

And there it is. End scene. Go the fuck home. Good job, Samantha. Way to bring up the ex-girlfriend while your tongue is practically down his throat. Maybe your next question should be about childhood traumas.

Brian didn't flinch. "A variety of reasons. We were in different places. Literally and figuratively. Plus, she wouldn't move here." He said it so matter-of-factly like he was reporting the weather.

"And you weren't prepared to move there?" I asked. Why? I have no idea. Blame it on my masochistic tendencies, but I persisted with my line of questioning.

"Nope. I have a job in IT, and I'm not leaving that opportunity to move up there," he replied, popping a tortilla chip into his mouth.

"You won't move to her, but you expect her to move to you?" I asked, arching an eyebrow.

He smiled at me coyly. "Hadn't thought about it that way, but yea, I guess so."

I stared at him. "True love is the act of loving someone else more than you love yourself," I blurted out.

Jesus Christ.

Who did I think I was, Confucius?

Brian blinked, slightly amused, slightly intrigued. Panic set in, and I immediately scrambled to recover. "Pretty sure I read that in a fortune cookie," I added, shoving another chip in my mouth to physically stop myself from talking.

His grin widened, and I exhaled in relief. He didn't seem to care that we were missing an entire party in the next room, didn't seem bothered by the fact that we were sitting on a cold bathroom floor, backs against the tub, talking about ex-girlfriends and philosophical fortune cookies.

It felt oddly easy. So I kept talking, and more surprisingly, he kept listening.

"I didn't cry at the funeral," I said softly, my voice dropping to that vulnerable place I hated.

Brian didn't move. Just watched me, his expression unreadable.

"I wanted to. But no tears came out." My cheeks flushed with embarrassment, but I didn't stop. "I was so mean to her before she died. I treated her like an inconvenience. I've never been more ashamed of myself."

His hand found mine, resting there, not gripping, not forcing comfort, just being there.

I swallowed. This was too much. The walls were crumbling, and I wasn't ready for that kind of collapse. So I did what I always did, I bailed on my own emotions.

"How are the two tallest people at the party fitting comfortably in a 4x4 bathroom?" I asked, forcing the air back into my lungs.

Brian smirked, giving me an out. "No clue. But I'd rather be in here with you than out there with anyone else."

My stomach flipped. Damn him.

"Smooth," I teased, snatching another chip.

The spare bedroom attached to the bathroom had a pull-out couch that was slightly too small, yet we managed to make it work, with the half-eaten bag of tortilla chips wedged between us like some kind of makeshift boundary. Not that we needed it.

We stayed up talking until I lost track of time, lost track the party, and lost track of the fact that I don't do this. I don't just *open up* to men I barely know. I don't let my guard down in the span of a single night. And yet, here I was.

And to be clear, all we did was sleep.

I woke up to the muffled sound of music blasting through the walls, a screamo band originating from Lee's room. My head was foggy, my throat dry from too many salty chips, and then—crinkle.

I immediately froze. Beneath my elbow was the unmistakable sound of a tortilla chip bag, and with horror, I realized I'd been using it as a pillow. Brian stirred beside me, still asleep, looking way too peaceful for someone who had been up talking until sunrise.

I needed to get out of here before he woke up and saw this hot mess express. I could feel the remnants of tortilla chips on my cheek and the taste of salt and Brian on my lips.

Slowly, I lifted my weight off the bed, peeling my arm away from the crinkled bag, and tiptoed toward the door like I was sneaking out of a heist.

I looked back at the bed, and the beautifully goofy male who laid on his back with his right arm tucked behind his head. His shirt was riding up slightly and I saw a hint of skin and a muscular V peeking out from between his t-shirt and jeans.

This perfect specimen. I bit back a smile.

Damn him. Again.

ele

After that night, it was a whirlwind. We were attached at the hip. Conversation, effortless, and chemistry, undeniable. I smiled morning, noon, and night, and for the first time in a long time, it didn't feel forced.

There was no guessing with Brian. No waiting by the phone or decoding texts. No bullshit ghosting or disappearing act. Just us, openly wanting each other in a stupidly refreshing way.

And we moved fast, very fast. Maybe too fast.

It had only been a week, and we already couldn't keep our hands off each other. It was constant, the stolen kisses, the late-night make-outs, the way my body buzzed just being near him.

But I was hesitant. Brian was so sweet and so new to all of this. He'd only ever been with one other girl, his ex, Karlie. And even though my own experience wasn't exactly scandalous, I couldn't shake the feeling that I was corrupting him.

That night, after a movie at Lee's, we raced back to my place, our usual ritual of teasing, kissing, and seeing how far we could push the line without crossing it.

Except tonight, the energy shifted. It was hungrier, less teasing, more needy.

His mouth was hot against my skin, his hands grasping harder, our bodies pressing together like we had something to prove. Feeling the tension in his body as his arms tightened around me, I pressed my entire frame into his, starting with my chest and heading south from there until even my core yearned to feel more of him. Even though he wore tattered denim jeans, I could feel what waited beneath them.

"You feel good," I murmured between kisses.

"So do you," he whispered, his breath warm against my neck.

I smirked. "Careful now, or I might just take advantage of you."

His hands tightened on my waist. "You can't take advantage of me if I'm consenting."

That's all it took. Clothes went flying, bodies connected, his mouth crushed against mine while he fumbled with my shirt, and before I could even process that *this was actually happening...*

It was happening. And then. Well. It happened.

It was over as quickly as it started, like a rollercoaster you waited an hour in line for, only to realize the entire ride lasted 30 seconds. Brian collapsed next to me, breathless, and grinning from ear to ear. I just stared at the ceiling, blinking.

And then immediately got the "ick."

⸺⁓⁓⸺

The next day, Georgia's voice was already at a pitch that suggested she knew exactly how this was going to go.

"It wasn't that good? Why the hell not?" she demanded, dramatically sipping her iced coffee.

I hesitated. "I can't put my finger on it."

"Well, apparently neither did he," she shot back, deadpan.

I chuckled. "I walked right into that one."

She shrugged, unfazed. "So, what, bad technique? Weird rhythm? Did he make that creepy eye contact thing the whole time? Did he cry? OMG, he cried, didn't he?"

I sighed. "I don't know. We just weren't in sync. Maybe I expected too much because up to this point, everything has felt incredible."

Georgia leaned forward, fully invested. "Dump him?"

I ugly cackled. "Bird, I'm not just going to dump him after one bad night of first-time sex. I mean, he's not that experienced so maybe he just needs to ride the bike more. Know what I mean? Take the training wheels off."

She squinted. "Dude, the only thing he should be riding is you, and if he can't do it well, then find someone who can."

"This is why you're single," I responded.

I wanted to play it cool. To act like one less-than-ideal night didn't make me question everything. But I'd be lying if I said Georgia's words didn't linger.

I hesitated. "Hopefully he's a quick learner."

Georgia snorted. "Sweetheart, that depends on the teacher."

Challenge accepted.

Thankfully, Brian was an exceptional student. And, with some unsolicited but shockingly useful advice from Lee, which I'll unpack in therapy at a later date, he went from tricycle to Harley Davidson in record time.

Crisis averted.

———ell———

Two weeks after Brian asked if I wanted to be exclusive, I was already getting cold feet. It wasn't him, not really. It was the fear creeping in, the gnawing feeling that he wasn't over Karlie, that I'd get too attached and he'd wake up one day and miss someone else more. And frankly, I wasn't sure I was over Lee.

So, naturally, I did the most mature, rational, emotionally intelligent thing possible.

I called Bobby.

I'm supposed to say I don't know why I called him. That it was a moment of weakness, a slip-up, an accident. But that would be a lie. I knew exactly why I called him.

I was setting fire to my own relationship before Brian had a chance to. Destroy before being destroyed. It wasn't a flawless strategy, but it was the only one I knew. And yes, casualties were inevitable. Mainly me.

Three minutes into Bobby being at my place, we were already kissing. And Bobby had this way of looking at me that short-circuited
my common sense. His eyes landed on me, and suddenly my body
forgot all the reasons why this was a terrible idea. I kissed him back.
Hard.

My hands tangled in his hair, his grip tightened at my hips, and I
was falling right back into him like no time had passed.

And then, something miraculous happened. I stopped, I actually
stopped. I pulled back, breath uneven, head spinning.

"I can't." The words tumbled out before I could second-guess
them. Bobby blinked, still holding onto me like I might change my
mind. "What?"

"I'm dating a great guy, and I don't want to screw it up."

A flicker of something unreadable in his expression. Then, disbelief.

"I miss you," he admitted, voice quieter than before. "I meant what
I said the other night, and I was hoping we could try this again."

My stomach twisted. He'd already confessed all of this to me one
drunken night out, and I should've resisted the urge to string him
along. Part of me still wasn't sure what or who I wanted. But in
this moment, it wasn't Bobby. He was too late. And I didn't think
this was payback for how he treated me—discarding me like I was
a piece of trash he could throw away. Honestly, I wasn't thinking

about Bobby's feelings at all. I was just trying to quiet the voices in my own head.

I swallowed. "I'm really sorry."

Bobby stared at me for a moment, and then, just like that, he knew.

He exhaled a small laugh, shaking his head. "He's a lucky guy. I hope he realizes how bitchin' you are. I guess I did, too late."

And then he left. Blue balls and all.

The guilt hit me instantly. Not for Bobby, for Brian. I picked up my phone and called him immediately, because if I didn't say it now, I knew I never would.

The second he answered, he said, "Whoa, that's weird. I was just about to call you."

I froze, gutted. I'm an idiot, such an idiot.

"I picked up my phone and it started ringing," he added. I let out a breath. My stomach tightened.

"Oh yeah?" I said, trying way too hard to sound normal. "Can't get enough of me?"

"Actually, I was at my parents' tonight, and I was telling them about my new girlfriend named Sam."

I sat up straighter. "Girlfriend, huh?"

He hesitated for the briefest moment, then, "Is that cool?"

I felt my guilt curl into something else entirely. Because at that moment, I realized I wasn't wavering anymore. I wanted Brian.

"Definitely," I said, smiling.

And just like that, Bobby became my little secret.

—ele—

We headed to a concert the next evening, my happy place. Something about loud guitars, pounding drums, and screaming nonsense into a mic settled my soul. It was pure chaos, and yet, it was the one thing that always made sense to me.

Brian liked my type of music too, which was a shockingly rare quality in a man, and something we did together often. But tonight felt different. The energy was buzzing between us all night.

Maybe it was the electricity of the crowd, or the way his hands found the front of my thighs every time the drums hit just right. Maybe it was just the way we kept looking at each other, longer than usual, heavier than usual.

By the time we left, I was lightheaded from the rush of it all.

Brian tossed me the keys to his Ram. "Think you can handle it?"

I rolled my eyes, catching them midair. "Please."

I drove us back to my place and expertly backed his truck into a tight parking spot in one smooth go.

Brian was silent for a beat. Then, with something close to reverence, he muttered, "That was hot."

I quieted the raging feminist monologue in my head and instead smirked. "What, you didn't think I could tame this beast?"

Brian exhaled a laugh, shaking his head. "Oh, I never doubted you."

But the way he was looking at me now, eyes dark, focused, hooded, was very different from the way he had looked at me five seconds ago. I barely had time to put the truck in park before his hands were on me. Fingers tangled in my hair. Lips crashed against mine. It was reckless and unhinged, like we had been holding back for too long and finally lost the battle.

I gasped into his mouth, the sound swallowed by his urgency. Brian pulled me over the center console, one hand gripping my thigh, the other bracing against the steering wheel as he pulled me into his lap.

"We should," I barely managed to get out.

"Yeah, I know." His mouth was already at my jaw, trailing heat down my neck.

"We should go inside."

"We should."

Neither of us moved. His hands skimmed my sides, fingertips dragging slowly, teasing, testing my resolve. I tilted my hips, and Brian cursed under his breath, gripping tighter.

"We're gonna get caught," he murmured, lips brushing my ear.

"No one's around." My voice was low and desperate.

His eyes met mine, dark and something more than just hungry. This was different. We weren't just rushing to get there anymore, we were choosing this. Deliberately.

His fingers traced the hem of my shirt, sliding beneath the fabric in a way that sent a shiver racing up my spine.

And then, everything else disappeared. The truck, the concert, the rest of the world. Just us, caught somewhere between too much and not enough.

His hands, exploring every square inch of me while his mouth traced a path of ecstasy and promise. Every touch, deliberate, and every moment, completely, undeniably real.

We didn't make it inside.

By the time we remembered to breathe, the windows were fogged, my pulse was still racing, and my body felt like it had just rewritten history. I blinked at him, still catching my breath. Brian let out a breathless laugh, grinning up at me. And in that moment, there was no more doubt. I had chosen him.

And he had just proven I'd made the right choice.

—

I barely managed to drag my suitcase inside, my body aching with exhaustion from the work trip, but the second I stepped through the door, I froze.

There, standing in the middle of my living room, was Brian. Holding roses and a handmade sign, slightly crooked, scrawled in his messy handwriting: "I missed you."

My brain took a solid five seconds to process what I was seeing. Wait, Brian had work tonight. He wasn't supposed to be here. But here he was.

I dropped my bag, heart flipping over itself, a grin already stretching across my face.

"What?" I started, then stopped, completely at a loss for words.

Brian shrugged, grinning like he hadn't just completely wrecked me.

"You were gone too long," he said simply.

I let out a half-laugh, half-sigh, walking straight into his arms, the scent of his cologne familiar and grounding. He was warm and solid. And in that moment, I knew, I had missed him so much it hurt. And it wasn't just the fun, flirty missing, the kind where you crave someone's texts, their presence, or their touch. It was deeper than that. It was the kind of missing that settles in your bones. The kind that whispers, "This person is becoming a part of you."

I looked up at him, the reality crashing over me all at once. This was real and so easy. This was love.

——*ele*——

Two months in, I did what I always did when things got too good, I panicked. It wasn't that I didn't like him, it was that I liked him too much. Loved him, actually. And if experience had taught me anything, it was this: when you care too much, you get burned. My friends saw it. My parents saw it. Hell, some random lady at the grocery store could probably see it.

It's too soon and he didn't have time to heal. You're going to be the rebound, and it's going to destroy you.

I heard all the voices in my head, nodding along like they were onto something. So, while mindlessly updating my iTunes, I called him to end it before he could.

"This isn't going to work out, Brian," I said, forcing my voice flat, detached, casual.

He froze. "What? Why? What did I do?"

I swallowed. "It's too soon. Let's be honest, you're not over Karlie."

Silence, and then the pushback.

"Sam," he said, voice low and steady. "I am over her. Trust me. I want to be with you and only you."

I hesitated at first, but then, caved because it was exactly what I wanted to hear. Was it the truth? At the time, I didn't even care.

The next night, Brian came over, and we did the only logical thing after a near breakup, we watched Dane Cook yell about Kool-Aid and bad relationships. Laughter was necessary.

We laid in bed, talking and laughing, and somewhere between a joke about *sangwiches* and mocking his dumb haircut from middle school, I realized it. I was so far gone for this boy.

And before I could stop myself I said those three little words. Right in the middle of a laugh, like it had been sitting on my tongue for weeks just waiting to slip out.

Brian froze. I froze.

Shit.

"What was that?" he asked, voice too damn soft for my current emotional spiral.

Shit!

I stared at him, wide-eyed, debating a full-on emergency evac-
uation from my bed.

SHIT!!

"Say it again," he said, smirking now, because he could smell my
panic. I swallowed hard, forcing my best defensive mask into
place.

"I said I love you, asshole"

Brian's lips curved into the kind of smile that could break a girl.

"Good," he murmured. Then a pause.

And just when my nerves were about to eat me alive, "Because
I love you too."

———— *ell* ————

The next morning, I called Georgia. I didn't even get a word
out before she screamed into the receiver.

"OH MY MOTHER-FUCKING GOD!"

"Jesus, Georgia. Volume."

"This isn't fair! Why do you always get the hot ones that are
awesome?!"

I grinned. "Wait, did you just call Bobby and Alec, hot and awesome?"

Ignoring me completely, she continued. "Well, you fucking suck," I could hear her pacing.

"But I love you. And I love you with him. And it's about damn time you picked someone that wasn't a giant twat. High five."

I laughed. "Twat. One of my favorite words, indeed. Let's go grab some celebratory mimosas."

"Screw mimosas. I'm getting some Jack."

"Georgia, you can't even stand the taste of anything stronger than a spritzer, and now you're drinking hard liquor?"

She corrected. "Jack is one of the bartenders."

I laughed. "Noted."

———

"You nervous?" Brian asked, grinning as he drove.

"Nah, parents love me," I said smoothly.

Lie.

Mothers, specifically, not so much. For whatever reason, I'd never had the best track record when it came to meeting parents. I wasn't rude or disrespectful. Hell, I thought I was extremely likable. And yet, Brian's mom proved my streak remained alive and well.

Dinner was fine. The food was good. His dad was pleasant. But his mother? Well, she kept referring to me as his friend. She also brought Karlie up as much as humanly possible for one evening.

"Oh, have you heard from Karlie lately?"
"How's Karlie doing these days?"
"Karlie always loved my cooking."

Cool. Awesome. Love that for me. It wasn't the worst parent encounter I'd ever had, but I also wouldn't be sending her a Mother's Day card.

By the time we left his parents' house and headed to our friend's party, I needed a drink. Or five. The night got better fast. It consisted of karaoke, flip cup, and far too much tequila. Brian was in a ridiculously good mood and I was soaking him up.

But the real turning point happened the moment I stepped out of the bathroom and found him waiting outside the door, with a devilish grin on his face. That look. I'd created that look, and I knew exactly what it meant. Oh boy, how I'd corrupted him.

I grabbed his hand and pulled him toward the nearest bedroom, pushing him inside without a second thought. Once the door shut, he was on me.

"Now, what am I going to do with you?" I teased, tilting my head in mock consideration.

"Whatever you please," he murmured, his lips finding my neck, hot and hungry.

Our mouths collided, tongues moving in a way that was so seamless, so familiar, it was almost unfair. His hands traveled everywhere, exploring like they were mapping territory that already belonged to him. Starting beneath my breasts, down my stomach, trailing lower. I shivered against him, heat pooling at every touch. He gripped my ass, squeezing tight and possessive. No, certain. Mine, and I was his. End of discussion.

He pulled back slightly, breathless, forehead against mine.

"Are we really doing this?"

Oh, don't start questioning things now.

"Don't bitch out on me, Brian," I whispered, nipping at his ear. That's all it took. In one move, he spun me around, unbuttoned his jeans, lifted my skirt, and—

God, It was fast. Fierce, like he needed it, like we needed it. I bit my lip, barely muffling the sounds threatening to escape. And then, as quickly as it started, it was over. Our chests rose and fell, our bodies still pressed together, neither of us wanting to move first. Then, reality hit.

We straightened our clothes, fixed our hair, tried to wipe the evidence off our faces, and crept out of the room, unnoticed.

Except, for the rest of the night, every time I caught Brian's eye, that cocky little grin was waiting for me. Evidence, written all over his face. And that smile, that goddamn smile.

It undid me every single time. This boy was going to be my undoing.

———*ele*———

It was a chilly, crisp night when my phone rang, and the sound of 'MakeDamnSure' filled the room.

I smiled instinctively. That was Brian's ringtone. I was curled up on my couch, next to the slightly cracked balcony door, the heat on full blast, letting in small ribbons of cool air. The contrast of warmth and crispness was my favorite sensation. A fire was burning somewhere in the neighborhood, the scent of woodsmoke and winter lingering in the air.

The night felt peaceful. And then I answered the call.

"Hey, good looking," I cooed, grinning like an idiot.

The silence that followed wasn't right. Then, his voice low, almost unrecognizable, "Hi."

A cold sensation crawled over my skin.

"Everything okay?" I asked.

A pause. "It's not something I want to talk about over the phone."

My stomach plummeted.

"I'm still coming over tonight," he continued. "We can talk then."

I could already hear it in his voice. I knew. **I knew.**

"Brian," I said, my voice turning flat and numb. "Just tell me."

A long, aching beat.

"I'm just, confused right now."

There it was. I stared straight ahead, watching the sheer curtain by the balcony ripple in the breeze.

"With us," I said, not even phrasing it as a question.

"Like I said," he muttered, "I'd rather talk in person."

I exhaled slowly, forcing my voice to stay neutral. "Whatever, that's fine."

The moment the call ended, the dam broke. Tears flooded my eyes so fast I could barely see my phone screen.

I called the only person I needed at that moment.

"Mom."

The second she answered, my breath hitched. "He's going to break up with me. I can feel it." And then, I just lost it. I unleashed everything, my insecurities and anxieties, every fear I hadn't even admitted to myself yet. It all came out in a frantic, breathless spiral. Because when I'm stressed, I don't just talk fast, I spin. Words tripping over each other, barely forming sentences, my thoughts racing too quickly for my mouth to catch up. I was spinning. Absolutely spinning.

"Oh, Sam," she murmured, instantly shifting into mom mode. "Take a breath. Calm down, sweetheart, it's going to be okay."

But we both knew she was lying. Nothing she could say would undo the pain already sinking into my stomach. Still, I let her words wash over me, trying to believe them.

I failed.

Once I hung up, and surely after giving her a mild heart attack, I sat there, motionless, just waiting. Stunned.

⁓ elle ⁓

Brian sat next to me on the couch. Too close, yet too far away.

We were wrapped in silence, the room filled with the distant hum of cars outside and the sharp tick of the clock on the wall. He couldn't even look at me.

"Sam, I'm really sorry," he said finally.

The words felt empty. I swallowed. "You said you loved me." My voice sounded wrong, distant, and detached.

He ran a hand over his face. "I know."

"So which is it? Do you love me or not?" I needed him to say it. One way or the other.

He opened his mouth, then closed it. Finally, he whispered, "Yes. I mean, I think. I'm not sure."

There it was, the knife. And still, I managed not to cry.

Because what was the point? What would it change? And I sure as shit wasn't going to give him the power at that moment.

He said goodbye, walked out the door, and that was that.

The second he left, the tears finally came. They flowed uncontrollably down my face. I dialed Georgia's number, choking on my own breath. She answered with zero hesitation.

"What up, hooker?"

All I could do was sob. Her voice immediately changed.

"Samantha. Babe. What's wrong?"

I tried to say it, but my words collapsed into each other, unintelligible through the sobs. Still, Georgia got the gist.

"WTF," she snapped. "How could he do this?!"

"I don't know," I managed. "I have no clue."

A pause, then, with absolute sincerity, "We ride at fucking dawn."

I sniffled. "Yea?"

"No, seriously," she continued. "Shovels, duct tape, bleach—we got this."

I should have laughed, I really should have, but humor was gone.

All that was left was agony.

⁓ℓℓℓ⁓

Words can't possibly describe how I felt that night.

But if I had to try, it was like swallowing fire. My stomach felt like I'd eaten an entire jar of carolina reapers. My body betrayed me. I was hot and cold at the same time, nauseous and starving, wide awake and exhausted.

I pulled my knees to my chest, arms wrapped around my legs, gasping for air like it physically hurt to breathe. The smell of the fire burning outside curled around me, and suddenly, I was back in this same position months ago when I lost my Nana. A new kind of grief but the same kind of pain.

And still, to this day, the smell of burning wood makes my chest ache.

The worst part of it all was that I spent weeks blaming myself. I'd lay in bed at times replaying every conversation, every date, every moment.

If only I had said this instead of that. If only I had been more patient. If only I had tried harder.

And every morning, I'd wake up from dreams where we were still together only to be slapped with the sickening realization that we weren't.

Until one day, I stopped blaming myself. And I finally saw the truth. It wasn't me, it wasn't me at all. It was him—his baggage, his unresolved bullshit. I had given him every opportunity to get out early. I had asked him, "Are you sure? Are you over her? Is this real?"

He was selfish. He still reeled me in, just long enough to hook me, before taking a gigantic gaff to my heart. I should've hated him. But I didn't, because some part of me still wanted to answer when he called. And for a while, I did.

Every evening, my phone would light up with his name, and I'd pick up without hesitation. We'd talk like nothing had changed, like he hadn't gutted me. But more importantly, like we were still us. I needed the communication. I craved it. I expected it. Hell, I relied on it.

Then the calls came less and less.

The first time he didn't call, I stayed up waiting. The second time, I checked my phone every ten minutes. The third, I texted first. By the fourth, I knew what was happening, the slow fade. And it was excruciating.

Then, one night, I realized I hadn't spoken to him in days. And then a week.

And then, for a couple of months, we didn't speak.

ele

The two-month silence should have been enough, but when Brian texted, "We're all going to Club BAX tonight, come with." I went. Because I was still stupid and I still wanted to prove something to him, or maybe to myself.

The club was loud, dark, and pulsing with bass. The kind of place where bad decisions felt like good ideas. I spotted Brian instantly, leaning against the bar, laughing with his friends, a drink in hand. And then I saw her. Some brunette with too much confidence and a dress short enough to be an invitation. She leaned into him, fingers tracing the length of his arm, whispering something in his ear.

And that's when it happened. The jealousy, the possessiveness, the rage. It was instantaneous, visceral, and completely unhinged. My brain checked out, like a switch flipped, and suddenly, I was moving. Marching straight toward them, heart pounding, blood boiling. People blurred past me, drinks sloshed over glasses as I shoved my way through the crowd, beelining for destruction.

I didn't even know what I was going to do. Snatch her hand away? Tell her to back the fuck off? Plant myself between them like a territorial psychopath? All I knew was that I was furious. And then Brian saw me, his eyes widened slightly, surprised to see me, or maybe surprised by whatever the hell was written on my face.

"Sam," he said, tilting his head, amusement flickering across his features.

Like this was cute. Like I was cute, and still wrapped around his finger.

The brunette blinked up at me, completely unbothered. "Um, hi?"

And that was it. I was right there, in her face. I didn't think or hesitate. I shoved between them, planting myself firmly in her space, my breath hot with adrenaline.

"The fuck did you say" I sneered, voice laced with something dangerous. The girl blinked at me, startled, confused, then immediately unimpressed.

"I—sorry, what?" she said, furrowing her brows, taking a step back.

I stepped closer.

"Did he tell you I was his girlfriend?" I asked, my voice low and sharp.

She frowned. "Uh... no? You have a girlfriend?" she asked, directing the question at Brian.

And before I could stop myself, I lunged.

Brian caught me mid-swing. His arms wrapped tight around my torso, pulling me back just as I nearly clawed this girl's face off.

"Sam, what the fuck?!" Brian barked, holding me firmly as I struggled against him.

I could feel people staring—my friends, his friends, her. All eyes on me.

The crazy ex-girlfriend.

And suddenly, it hit me. The moment I saw myself from the outside. What the fuck was I doing? I wasn't his girlfriend. I wasn't even his problem. I was just a girl he used to date, now losing her goddamn mind in the middle of a club over a guy who had already left.

The realization hit me so hard, that I stopped fighting. Brian felt it too, the way my body went slack in his arms.

I turned my head, eyes meeting his. And the look on his face was something that would haunt my dreams forever: pity.

I hated him for that. Shit, I hated myself for that. Without another word, I tore myself from his grip and walked straight out of the club.

Didn't say goodbye. Sure as hell didn't check my phone when he texted five minutes later.

Because I knew, this was my breaking point. This was the moment I took my power back.

———ele———

I stood in my garage, staring at the sad, beat-up dresser I'd found on the side of the road last week. It had good bones, a little charm, and years of potential ahead of it.

Too bad the same couldn't be said for my most recent relationship.

Sighing, I dragged the sander across the old wooden dresser, bracing myself for a long afternoon of emotional destruction. I should be crying. Should be curled up under a blanket, binge-watching terrible reality TV. Figure out what Johnny Bananas is up to these days.

I ran my hand over the wood and smiled. A blank slate. If this dresser had feelings, it would have filed a restraining order by now.

At least the dresser didn't make excuses. Didn't ghost me, then show up seven weeks later with a half-assed *"Hey, we should hang."*

With every pass, I imagined the rough edges smoothing out, the chipped paint disappearing beneath the force of my frustration. The sander vibrated in my grip, a steady hum of controlled destruction, and I let the rhythmic motion take over.

If only heartbreak worked the same way. If only I could just sand it down until it was nothing but raw wood, stripped of its past mistakes, ready for a fresh coat of something new, something better.

The air filled with dust and pent-up frustration, and honestly, it was cathartic as hell. I wiped my forehead with the back of my wrist, leaving a streak of dust across my temple.

I exhaled, stepping back to examine my work. The dresser wasn't perfect yet, patchy spots remained, stubborn imperfections refusing to budge, but it was getting there, ready for a fresh start.

And maybe, so was I.

———ele———

It was Halloween, which meant I was dressed in something that barely qualified as clothing. In my defense, I wasn't alone in my questionable life choices, half the city was wearing fishnets and bad decisions.

And tonight, I felt invincible. Brian was a thing of the past. I could officially say that now. It had been about 8 months since the night at Club-BAX.

We still talked sometimes, flirty texts and the occasional run-in, but I never gave him my full attention anymore, and I could tell it was driving him insane.

Which is probably why, as I stood at the bar chatting with a very cute stranger, my phone lit up with his name. *Brian.*

"Come to Lee's."

I stared at the screen, rolling my lip between my teeth. Proctologist hottie or Brian? Who wins tonight?

I wish I could say I debated it. That I made the responsible choice, but I didn't. I went to Lee's.

Lee's house was the same as always, crowded, loud, slightly sticky. And then there was Brian, standing in the doorway, a slow, knowing grin spread across his face the second his eyes locked onto mine.

His gaze dropped over the dangerously short hem of my outfit, down to the fishnets hugging my thighs. The heat in his stare sent a pulse straight through me.

"Cute costume," he murmured as I brushed past him.

I didn't respond. I just let my fingertips trail the length of his chest as I passed and that was all it took. Immediately, his hand was around my wrist, tugging me through the house, past the drunken mascots, and into a darkened spare room.

And what happened next, well, it wasn't sweet or gentle. Certainly, wasn't love. It was something entirely different. It was rough and quick, but mostly, it was final. Like neither of us was really here, just chasing something that used to exist, grasping at the past for one last taste.

Hands against the wall. Breathless, reckless movements. No words, just nails dragging, hands gripping, teeth scraping.

For the first time, there were no feelings left to protect, and maybe that's why it felt so different. Because this wasn't us anymore. This was two people who used to be something, burning off the last of whatever was left.

The next morning, Brian was still passed out on the bed. And me, I was already gone. The only proof I had ever been there? A pair of torn fishnets tossed on the rug. A set of handcuffs abandoned on the floor.

And a ghost of a memory that wouldn't follow me out the door.

Shane: The Heartthrob

"Wicked Games – by Jessie Villa"

We met on Halloween at a bar. I was dressed as a devil, not the kind that implied subtlety, a barely-there pleated skirt, boy-short underwear (yes, that's how short the skirt was), and a black corset that left little to the imagination. The only thing actually *devilish* about my costume was the set of red horns perched on top of my head.

And honestly, that was enough.

I was living my best single life. Making bad decisions in the best kind of way. And tonight, given my attire, I had an added dose of confidence running through my veins.

Then *he* walked by. Tall, sun-kissed, wearing a white medical coat with a fake plastic butt sewn to the back. A proctologist costume.

Jesus Christ.

His bright blue eyes and electric smile could cure cancer, and he fucking knew it.

As he passed, I reached out, pinching the plastic cheek of his costume and winking up at him. He stopped short, confused. His eyes roamed, slow, deliberate, taking in every last inch of me.

"A devil indeed," he murmured, his expression caught somewhere between amusement and something else.

I noticed his gaze flicker toward the bar. Another guy was standing there, watching him.

Ohhhhhhhh.

"Whoops. My mistake," I said, raising an eyebrow and jerking my chin toward his friend. "Didn't realize you were spoken for."

He blinked. "Wait, what?"

"You like men," I said with a casual shrug, knowing damn well he didn't, given how he undressed me with his eyes.

"No, I'm not—I mean, uh, no. That's not—" He was stuttering, trying to process whatever the hell this interaction was, and I just grinned, sipping my drink, watching him flail.

It was adorable. I had him gobsmacked, and I was enjoying every second of it.

"Go get him, tiger." I finished and started to walk away.

For a second, he just stared at me, then he quickly grabbed my arm. God his hands felt good on my skin.

"I'll be right back," he said suddenly, snapping out of his haze. "Don't go anywhere."

Hmmm. What's a girl to do? I could've stayed put and made his life easier.

Or...

I could disappear into the crowd, find another poor soul to torment, and if he was hungry enough, he'd come find me.

I chose the latter.

I made my way to the bar, sipping my drink, feigning disinterest, waiting to see if he'd hunt me down, and it didn't take long.

Out of the corner of my eye, I saw him approaching. And because I'm an asshole—and because I knew exactly what I was doing—I took that moment to shamelessly bend over, and adjust my fishnets where they had tangled at the tops of my boots.

I knew he was watching. I wanted him to watch. And I wasn't disappointed.

The moment I straightened, I felt his presence behind me, close enough that I could hear the deep exhale through his nose. I knew what I was doing, I was toying with him and I couldn't help myself. It's not like this was going to lead to anything. He was some random guy at a bar and I certainly wasn't the type to take home strays. But shit, while I was here, I could at least make him sweat a bit. Besides, I needed some late-night amusement.

"Need a hand," he smirked.

I chuckled, turning to face him. "I don't know what you're talking about."

His blue eyes sparkled with something playful. "I think you do."

And, maybe I did.

Our conversation wasn't particularly memorable, something about our costumes, something about how absurd the whole night was. But those eyes? That smile? That was memorable as hell.

Six feet tall. Built, but not too built. The kind of body that came from surfing or some other relaxed-but-athletic lifestyle. Piercing, and I mean, *piercing* blue eyes, with a lethal, panty-melting grin. He was good-looking and he knew it. The type of guy who had been with a lot of women.

You could tell by the way he carried himself. The easy confidence and swagger. The way he didn't even have to try. He was definitely my type, which meant I should steer clear.

By the end of the night, he was eating out of the palm of my hand. We exchanged numbers even though I had no intention of texting him, and as I entered his number in my phone, another text came through.

I smirked. Then I walked out, but not because I was going home, because I had one last stop to make.

Somewhere familiar, with another man waiting for me, handcuffs ready.

~ele~

He called a few days later. I'll admit, I was a little surprised to see his name pop up on my phone. I had barely given him a second thought since that night.

Guys like Shane were a dime a dozen. Hot, cocky, smooth talkers who knew how to flirt and had a Rolodex of women on speed dial.

Still, I figured, why not? We settled on sushi, his choice and a solid pick at that. Showed he had taste, and he wasn't just another beer-and-wings kind of guy.

He got there first, securing a table, which gave me the perfect opportunity to make a grand entrance.

Truthfully, I couldn't even remember exactly what he looked like. I knew he was hot, obviously, I had standards. I could recall his ridiculous Halloween costume, the absurd plastic butt, and that smug, heart-stopping smile. Mostly, I remembered the way he carried himself, like a man who knew exactly how good-looking he was. But beyond that, it was all a little fuzzy.

What wasn't fuzzy, however, was the look on his face when I walked through the door—mouth open, eyes wide, and I think I heard him gasp.

I strutted through the entrance, my low-rise jeans hugging my hips perfectly, a sliver of bare stomach on display, my black crop turtleneck clinging to my curves just enough to make him sweat. I wasn't even looking at him yet, but I felt his reaction. That sharp inhale, the way his whole body shifted toward me like I had my own gravitational pull. He stood instinctively to greet me. Manners. Noted.

By the time I reached the table, his lips had parted slightly, his expression unreadable, and I swore I heard a quiet, almost whispered, "Damn."

Got him.

Shane blinked, exhaled what seemed like relief, and shook his head as if trying to clear his thoughts. "You," he huffed, dragging a hand down his face, "I couldn't remember what you looked like."

I smirked, reaching for the menu even though I already knew what I wanted. "Hopefully you guessed that I'm not actually the devil."

Shane let out a breath, his gaze flicking over me like he was still recalibrating. "That's still to be determined."

Indeed.

I hummed, flipping open the menu. He laughed, shaking his head like he wasn't sure if he was thrilled or terrified.

We talked about a lot and nothing all at once. He worked for the government, had a yellow lab named Maya, and he loved fishing and boating. Anything that got him on the water. He grew up in Florida and his parents divorced when he was eight. His job brought him to Virginia.

He was nice enough. Funny, but not in a trying-too-hard kind of way. He had an ease about him, that lazy confidence some men just had, the kind that said *I know I'm attractive, but let's pretend I don't for fun.*

And yet, I didn't try too hard with him. Not because I wasn't enjoying myself, he was good company, but I was seeing two other guys at the time, and I had a firm policy of not putting all my eggs in one basket.

And if I had learned anything about men like Shane, the less effort I put in, the harder he was going to chase.

And judging by the way his eyes kept locking onto mine, the way he leaned in just a little closer every time I spoke, the way his fingers absently toyed with the edge of his napkin like he was itching to touch something.

Yeah.

He was already hooked.

———*ele*———

Shane invited me to a work event. It was still early, new enough that neither of us had officially put a label on whatever the hell this was,

but exclusive enough that he damn well should've known better than to pull what he did.

I walked in, expecting a normal night of flirtation and vali-
dation, only to be met with a sight that had me damn near
choking on my own breath.

Shane had three other women with him. **Three.**

Like some kind of Bachelor contestant who didn't realize the
cameras weren't rolling.

At first, I thought maybe I had misread the situation. Maybe
these were his coworkers, some mutual friends, someone's random plus-one.

But no. These were his guests, his invitees—his dates.

*Oh. **Oh.***

I took a slow breath, plastering on my best unbothered
face, even though my brain was lighting up with sirens. Red
flag, abort mission. This was a massive, screaming, some-
one-get-this-man-a-psych-evaluation, red flag. Except, instead
of running, I saw it for exactly what it was: a challenge.

Because here's the thing, I wasn't jealous, not even a little.
And not because I was some cool, enlightened, totally secure
woman. No. It was because none of these women stood a
chance.

I had already won, they just didn't know it yet. And neither did Shane.

Game on.

—— ℓℓ ——

If Halloween had been my seductive devil era, tonight was my celestial revenge arc. Gone was the pleated barely-there skirt, devil horns, the knee-high boots, and the "yes I know exactly what I'm doing" smirk.

Tonight, I was ethereal. My dress was soft, and flowing, the kind of material that clung in all the right places but still looked effortless, like I had descended from a cloud rather than my car in the parking lot.

My makeup was angelic and innocent, nothing like what I actually was, a walking contradiction to the thoughts running through my mind. Because while I may have looked like heaven...

I was about to make Shane burn for me.

—— ℓℓ ——

The night unfolded as expected, Shane, ever the charmer, moved between his guests, making conversation, laughing at jokes that weren't that funny, playing the role of Mr. Popular.

I, however, played my own role. I didn't sulk or pout. Didn't act like the woman scorned.

Instead, I shined.

I tossed my hair at all the right moments, laughed effortlessly, and flirted just enough with some of his coworkers, trying to understand the lure Shane had. I laid the charm on, thick, and radiated the kind of confidence that didn't demand attention, it commanded it.

Shane noticed. Oh, did he notice. He was tracking every move I made.

He might have walked in with four women tonight, but this wasn't a fair chess game. I was the queen, and he was just another king I was about to take off the board, he just didn't know it yet.

Every time I caught his gaze from across the room, his eyes darkened just a little more. His fingers flexed at his sides like he was resisting the urge to reach for me. He wasn't as smooth anymore, wasn't as focused on whatever surface-level conversation he was having.

He was unraveling, and I just smiled.

By the end of the night, it was clear, Shane had walked into this event with four women at his side, but he was leaving with only one.

Me.

It was me he led out the door. It was me he pressed up against the car, hands sliding down my back, and up my dress, his breath hot against my throat. It was me he practically undressed, his fingers working at the layers beneath my dress as if he were unwrapping some forbidden gift.

And it was me, only me, who sealed the deal.

Because let's be honest.

There was never any other option.

—ele—

The car ride back to his place was magnetic, silent but thick with the unspoken. The kind of silence that wasn't uncomfortable, but electric, like neither of us wanted to break the tension because we both knew where it was leading.

Then, the opening chords of 'MakeDamnSure' by Taking Back Sunday crackled through the radio speakers. I tensed, my stomach twisted. Nope, not tonight.

Before the first lyric could land its punch, I reached forward and slammed the preset button, switching to another station.

Shane's eyes flicked to me, amused. "Not a fan?"

"Not in the mood," I muttered, staring out the window, pretending I hadn't just been sucker-punched by the ghost of an ex-boyfriend I refused to name.

Shane didn't press, just nodded, fingers tapping against the steering wheel, that small smirk still tugging at the corners of his mouth.

Then those same fingers landed ever so gently on my thigh. As if he knew he needed to redirect my attention. He wasn't about to lose this moment between us and where it was heading. As if on cue, the tension simmered back to where it had been, thick and crackling between us. I let my eyes drift to his mouth. Let my mind wander to what I'd be doing with it later.

And by the time we got inside, it was game over. The door had barely clicked shut before he had me backed against it, his breath warm against my cheek. His hands cupped my ass, fingers pressing just hard enough to send a shiver down my spine, claiming what was his.

"You knew exactly what you were doing tonight," he murmured, his lips hovering near my ear.

I smirked, tilting my head slightly. "Did I?"

"You're playing a dangerous game," he exhaled a laugh, shaking his head like he couldn't believe it, like he couldn't believe me. He'd met his match.

"Check mate," I responded.

And then we collided. His lips devoured mine, all heat and hunger like he'd been holding back all night, and finally, finally let himself snap. I let him. Hell, I welcomed it. His hands roamed with purpose, fingertips pressing into my hips, my back, my thighs. I could feel the heat rolling off of him, the way his body pressed flush against mine, how the firm grip of his hands made it clear that whatever restraint he had shown earlier was now a distant memory. And I had been the one to break him.

I wrapped my arms around his neck, pulling him closer, deepening the kiss until there was nothing left between us but breathless anticipation. His tongue traced along my bottom lip, slow and teasing, his fingers inching up my spine, leaving a trail of fire in their wake.

His eyes darkened, a flicker of something dangerous, something raw passing over his features before his hands lifted me effortlessly, legs wrapping around his waist as he carried me further into the room.

There was nothing hesitant about him. Nothing unsure, and I liked that.

Shane wasn't asking for permission and he wasn't second-guessing himself. He was taking what he wanted. Taking what we both knew had been inevitable since the moment I laid my hands on his ridiculous plastic butt at the bar. This had been a slow burn. A game I had set into motion and let unfold in real time.

And now, it was game over.

I let my head fall back, let my body sink into his as his lips continued their descent down my neck, let myself get lost in the feeling
of being wanted like this.

Shane wasn't soft or careful. He wasn't treating me like some
delicate thing to be cherished. No, Shane was consuming me. And
I let him.

Because tonight, that was exactly what I wanted.

———ele———

He told me his ex-girlfriend was coming back into town. Just for
a few nights to organize a birthday event for him and *their* mutual
friends. Just long enough to remind me that, despite how he treated me behind closed doors, I was still not invited into certain parts
of his world.

That should have been the biggest red flag. A giant, neon, flashing
RUN, BITCH sign. But Shane tended to be the peacekeeper,
which, in reality, meant he was a master at keeping people happy
by never actually making a decision. And in doing so, he didn't set
boundaries.

"She just wants to put something together for the group," he explained, running a hand through his hair like he already knew this
conversation was a minefield.

I leaned against the counter, arms crossed. "Right. For the group."
"Yeah."
"And I am, what? A threat to the delicate ecosystem of this friend group?"
He sighed. "It's not like that."
"Really, because it feels like that."

Shane was a lot of things. He was hot, charismatic, and a walking temptation wrapped in a smile that made girls stupid. But was he confrontational? Nope.

If he had a mantra, it would have been "Let's not make this a thing." Except, this *was* a thing.

He went out that night while I stayed home. It was fine. Until it wasn't.

At first, we were texting. Nothing over the top, nothing clingy, just casual check-ins. Then, around midnight...Radio. Fucking. Silence.

I gave him the benefit of the doubt. For about an hour. By 1 a.m., I was side-eyeing my phone, wondering if he had accidentally died. By 2 a.m., I had gone full FBI investigation mode. Was he okay? Had his phone died? Did he drink too much and pass out?

Or, the most obvious answer, was he exactly where I thought he was? The question sat like acid in my stomach. I hated it. Hated that I even cared enough to entertain the idea that he was somewhere he shouldn't be.

I clenched my teeth, exhaled through my nose, and did the very thing I told myself I wouldn't do. I got in my car and drove straight to his place. I knocked, waited, and nothing happened. Knocked again, only to be met by more silence.

My jaw clenched so hard I was at risk of cracking a molar, but I refused to let my anger morph into something worse, something pathetic. I wasn't about to stand on his doorstep, looking like a desperate girlfriend who needed answers.

So, I turned around, got in my car, and drove home in silence, gripping the wheel like it could somehow ground me. What the hell was I doing? This was absurd. I was slipping into the same needy, obsessive patterns I'd sworn I'd outgrown. Except, I had moved on from that behavior.

At 3 a.m., still nothing. By 4 a.m., the anger was gone. I wasn't hurt or sad. I was just, done.

I had already written him off and by noon, there was a knock at the door. I ignored it. I wasn't expecting anyone, and I wasn't in the mood to reject salvation today. Another knock and then the doorbell.

For fuck's sake.

I ripped the door open with a sigh. "I don't need the Lord, our Savior, in my heart."

And then stopped short. *Shane.*

I scowled. "Ugh. You're worse than a Jehovah's Witness."

And then I slammed the door in his face. I barely made it two steps before it swung open behind me. I cursed under my breath. *Should've locked it.*

Shane walked in like he owned the place, running a hand through his hair with a long exhale. "Okay, first of all, my phone broke."

I arched an eyebrow but didn't say anything. He held up both hands like he was surrendering. "I swear. Screen shattered. Couldn't call, couldn't text."

Still, I didn't react. Didn't move or flinch. He let out a humorless, panicked laugh. "I was shit-faced, Sam. No phone. No way to get in touch with you. Barrett had to drag me back to his place before I did something stupid, like try to drive home."

I kept my expression unreadable, but I hated that some part of me wanted to believe him. I let the silence stretch.

Finally, after what felt like an eternity, I lifted my gaze, my voice slow and deliberate. "Your phone broke. You were too drunk to drive. No one had my number. And your only option was to sleep at Barrett's?"

He nodded. "That about sums it up."

I studied him, reading every inch of his face, every micro-expression.

"So, you spent the night with Barrett. Not her?" The question burned my throat.

"Absolutely not, Sam," he said, his voice firm. "I don't want to be with anyone but you."

That was all it took. Against my better judgment, I believed him. And just like that, he kicked off his shoes, pulled his shirt over his head, and collapsed onto my bed. Collapsed like he belonged there. And I let him.

Still confused if this meant we were exclusive, but mostly I was still uneasy from the night before. He fell asleep within minutes, deep, unbothered, peaceful sleep. Like his night hadn't just unraveled me at the seams.

Up until this point, I had no reason to second-guess him. Everything was fine. There was no need to make a mental movie or to self-sabotage. Definitely, no need to trust my gut.

Right?

———

The next morning, I called the only person who would tell me the truth, no matter how much I didn't want to hear it. Georgia picked up on the third ring.

"It's too early for whatever dumbass decision you made last night," she greeted, voice still raspy with sleep.

"I think I'm being an idiot," I whispered.

A long pause. Then, the sound of shuffling sheets.

"Go on," she said, suddenly wide awake. Georgia lived for my bad life choices.

I sighed, pressing my palm to my forehead. "Shane disappeared last night. Didn't answer his phone. No texts, no calls, just gone. So I did what any sane, completely rational person would do and drove to his place at two in the morning."

"Classic."

"I know," I groaned.

"And what, exactly, did you discover on your quest, Lois," she said, half amused, half exasperated.

"Well, nothing. He didn't answer. I was convinced he had been kidnapped, or murdered, or—"

"Balls deep in someone else?"

Silence.

Georgia sighed. "So what's his excuse?"

I swallowed. "He showed up at my door at noon and said his phone broke. That he was too drunk to drive and no one had my number. So basically, Barrett dragged him to his house before he did something stupid."

More silence.

Then, a sharp inhale.

"And you believed him?"

I hesitated. That was all she needed.

"Jesus Christ, Sam."

"What? What was I supposed to do? He showed up, looking all disheveled and miserable."

"And you let him in? Christ, you're such a sucker for a good-looking man with a convenient excuse."

I groaned. "His phone was shattered. He didn't drive drunk. No one had my number. I mean, it was kind of valid."

"Is it really?"

I bit my lip.

Georgia sighed, her voice softer now. "Look. I get it, I do. You like him, and maybe he's telling the truth. Maybe his phone really did break, and he did pass out at Barrett's. But you're not mad because he disappeared. You're mad because it felt familiar."

I inhaled sharply. She wasn't wrong.

"This is Bobby and Alec and Lee all over again," she continued. "You're replaying the same game, hoping for a different ending. So

I need you to ask yourself something, Sam, if Shane weren't Shane, if this was anyone else, would you still be this understanding?"

I didn't answer. Because we both knew the truth.

"That's what I thought," Georgia said. "Now, get up, get dressed, and remind yourself that you're hot as fuck and don't need to be waiting by the door for some dude to remember he's lucky to have you."

I exhaled a small laugh. "You're insufferable."

"I know. But you love me."

"I do."

"Good. Now, go make him sweat a little."

———

Shane spent most of his free time down at the docks. It was his second home, where he killed time, where he tinkered with boats that weren't his, where he shot the shit with the same guys he'd known for a decade.

I'd agreed to meet him for lunch today at a restaurant on the docks. I'd been playing it cool for a few weeks now. Georgia's words still rang in my head—*Make him sweat a little.*

He would text me and I'd text back if I felt like it. We still hung out, mostly at his place, and I'd stay as long as I wanted, leaving when

I was bored. Sometimes I sat on the couch, scrolling my phone, completely unbothered. Sometimes I barely acknowledged him. It was a full-blown gambit. And it was working.

He thought he was running the game, the smooth player keeping his options open, but in reality, I was three moves ahead, waiting for him to realize there was only ever one winning strategy—me. It was an art and a science, really. And it was working, because Shane was fucking unraveling.

At first, it was subtle. The way he'd glance at me when I wasn't looking, abandon whatever task he was pretending to be busy with the second I showed up, or the way his shoulders would tense when I got up to leave too soon.

But then, it wasn't subtle at all.

This particular day, I walked up to find him mid-conversation with one of his dock friends, talking about God knows what. I wasn't listening. I was too busy pulling my hair into a ponytail, tying it up casually and effortlessly. Like I didn't notice the way Shane's eyes darkened immediately.

And then, as if that wasn't enough, I took off my sunglasses slowly, the kind of slow that suggested I wasn't in a rush for anything. I barely even looked at him, and yet, he was practically vibrating with frustration.

"You're doing this on purpose," he said, his voice gruff.

I turned my head slightly, blinking at him like I had no idea what he was talking about.

"Doing what?"

His friend snorted, looking between us. "I'm gonna go anywhere else."

Smart man.

Once we were alone, Shane let out a breath and dragged a hand down his face. He was exasperated and frustrated. Practically foaming at the mouth.

"Alright," he said, stepping closer. "You win."

I arched a brow. "Excuse me?"

His jaw clenched and his hands landed on his hips. I watched him carefully, the way his patience was thinning and his cool composure was slipping. Shane, the ever-chill, ever-casual playboy, was losing his damn mind.

"You heard me." He exhaled sharply, staring at me like I was the most maddening thing he'd ever encountered. "I'm done playing whatever game you think we're playing."

I made a show of taking a slow sip of my iced coffee. "Maybe I like games."

Shane let out a humorless laugh and shook his head, pacing for a second before finally stopping in front of me.

"Sam," he said, voice lower now. "Enough. I don't want to do this whole 'casual' thing anymore."

I lifted my chin slightly, watching him. And there it was, the shift. The moment he cracked before I did and made it official before I even had to ask. The satisfaction was sweet.

"That means what, exactly?" I challenged, just to make him sweat a little more.

Shane groaned, dragging a hand through his hair before stepping even closer, invading my space, and forcing me to tilt my chin up.

"You're mine, Sam," he muttered. "No more games. No more wondering. Mine."

And maybe, that's exactly what I wanted to hear, so I smirked, tilted my head, and in the most nonchalant, maddeningly frustrating tone possible, I said, "If you insist."

Then, I walked away, leaving Shane standing there, fists clenched, ready to combust.

—*ele*—

Shane was coming back from a trip and needed a ride home from the airport.

We'd been going strong for a couple of months now, long enough to make plans to visit his family in Florida, but not quite long enough to say, "I love you."

Not yet. But when we were together, it was kismet. Smiling from ear to ear, unable to stop touching, constantly pulling each other closer like we existed in our own gravitational force.

So, naturally, I decided to spice up his homecoming and I showed up at the arrivals hub in a khaki trench coat, and nothing else.

It was bold and ridiculous. It was very *me*.

I stood there casually, scrolling through my phone like I wasn't half-naked in a very public place, while travelers bustled around me, oblivious. Then, I spotted him. Shane was walking toward me, duffle bag slung over his shoulder, scanning the crowd. His gaze landed on mine, and instantly, his expression shifted. His smirk, the one that said, I-don't-know-what-you're-up-to-but-I-like-it, was plastered across his face.

His eyes flicked down, taking in the trench coat and his brow lifted. Oh, he knew. The second he reached me, he leaned in, voice low, teasing.

"Aren't you a little warm in a jacket?"

I tilted my head. "Depends."

"On?"

I stepped closer, my lips ghosting over his ear as I whispered, "On how fast you can get me out of it."

I barely got the words out before he grabbed my hand, already leading me toward the exit. The ride back to his place was charged with tension. Every red light felt like an eternity, and each glance he stole at me was thick with anticipation. When I shifted, the hem of my coat barely covered my thighs, his grip on the wheel tightened.

By the time we made it inside, we didn't even make it past the entryway. The door clicked shut and then it was hands, mouths, and clothes (or in my case, just *one* article of clothing) being discarded as we crashed into each other.

I loved this part of us. The ease and playfulness. The way it was no pressure, all fun, entirely us. It was glorious.

He laid me on the bed and I watched as his gaze caressed me up and down. Starting at my heavy blue eyes, then slowly hovering along the top of my firm breasts, down my stomach, and lingering right at the core of me. As if answering to my heat, he knelt at the edge of the bed, grabbed my hips, and pulled me toward him.

He kissed my inner thighs gently but intentionally, and then softly moved to the center. He buried his face into my core licking, sucking, kissing—claiming. He repeated again and again until he had me at the peak of ecstasy. My entire body tightened and then in one blissful moment, I released, moaning as my climax shattered through me.

I was just barely coming down from my high when I felt him plunge into me. With one swift motion, he was moving in and out of me, a rhythm that wasn't rehearsed but private to only us. I went over the edge, again and again.

And then, at some point in the tangled mess of limbs and lips and passionate releases, the words slipped out.

Three little words. Completely unplanned.

I didn't even realize I'd said them until I heard them. The moment hung between us, suspended in the air. His breath stilled and so did mine. My heart hammered.

Fuckity, Fuckity, Fuck.

I could've played it off and backtracked, laughed it away like it was just a product of heat and adrenaline. But we both knew better. I meant it.

And now, there was no taking it back.

——ele——

Things with Shane were moving. Not fast, but not slow. Just that awkward middle speed where you confess your love and he doesn't reciprocate. So somewhere in that hazy space between casual and committed, I found myself saying yes when Lee asked me to the firefighter ball.

We hadn't seen each other in a while, but we kept in touch, always orbiting, like two planets that never quite collided. He needed a date and I needed a night that reminded me of who I was before all of the overthinking and waiting.

The firefighter ball was elegant and charming. Like stepping into a world that didn't expect anything from me except to smile and clink glasses. And Lee was warm, attentive, and familiar. There was no pressure, no games. Just comfort.

I told myself it was just a favor for an old friend. But truthfully, I knew it meant more than that. Enough to make me question whether Shane was giving me what I actually needed.

Lee even threw me the curveball of the century. And my response was to completely shut down hoping that avoidance would make the confusion disappear.

I packed for my Florida trip with Shane, trying to stay focused. However, I felt it. The familiar twist in my gut. The whisper of doubt.

And just like that, my head was no longer sure. But worse, neither was my heart.

The trip to meet his family had been planned for weeks. I had a work event near Shane's hometown, and since we were already making the trip, we figured, why not meet his parents. Officially.

It wasn't a huge deal. I'd met parents before. And every time, it went spectacularly wrong.

Craig's family? Hated me.
Brian's mother? She practically clutched her pearls the second I walked through the door.
Alec's parents? Nice enough. But that meeting turned him into a different individual entirely and I still had PTSD as a result.

And on top of that, Shane still hadn't said *I love you* back. Not that I was keeping score or obsessing over it. Not that every time we were together, I wasn't waiting for it, listening for it, hoping it would slip out in some unguarded moment.

Nope. Not at all. Totally chill over here.

Instead of saying it, he showed it through little things, like pulling me into his lap absentmindedly, as if it were second nature, or looking at me in a way that suggested he was seeing something he wasn't quite ready to admit. Then there was the way he'd kiss me in the little secret spot I'd never let any other boyfriend explore (outside of Craig).

So, for now, I let it go.

Besides we were in Florida, and the first stop was meeting his mother.

———ℓℓ———

It was lunch, it was pleasantries, and it was keeping my natural tendency toward sarcasm in check for an hour or two. Easy.

She wasn't bad, but she wasn't great, either. She was warm, but not too warm, pleasant, but not overly pleasant. She gave me a polite smile, asked the usual questions, and made small talk in a way that felt practiced rather than genuine. She was fine.

A solid 6 out of 10 on the Meet-the-Parents scale. She wasn't throwing daggers or clutching pearls, which, for me was basically a win.

By the time lunch ended, I wasn't dreading spending more time with her, but I also wasn't ready to add her on Facebook.

———ℓℓ———

After lunch, we decided to enjoy the warm Florida weather and borrowed a friend's 18' center console, stocked a cooler with drinks, and took off into the Intracoastal. And if there was one thing I knew about Shane, it was that the man lived for the water. It was his religion, his reset button. The place where his mind slowed down and everything made sense.

The sun was high, the water calm, and the salt clung to my skin in that perfect, lazy Florida way.

It was one of those effortless days. There were no timelines or expectations. Just the sun, the wind, and us. We drifted around and swam a bit. We lay on the deck, drinking cold beer and letting the heat bake into our skin. And, naturally, because I was me and he was him, things escalated. I don't know who started it.

Maybe it was him, fingers trailing along my thigh while we drifted. Maybe it was me, shifting onto his lap, my bikini still wet from the water. Or maybe it was the heat, the quiet, the fact that we were out there alone, no one in sight.

All I know is somewhere between floating on our backs and cracking open another drink, I found myself riding him, his hands gripping my ass. The sun beat down on my back, warming my skin, the scent of salt and sunscreen lingering in the air. The boat rocked beneath us, each gentle sway making every movement more intense, every breath more charged.

I rocked back and forth, savoring the moment of ecstasy and peaceful bliss. And when we were both on the verge of climax, I grabbed his shoulders and pressed down ensuring maximum pleasure. Our moans probably sent the fish swimming for cover, but being the only two souls for miles made it utterly exhilarating. Just me, Shane, and the endless stretch of crystal blue, where the sea and sky blurred into infinity.

And it was absolutely perfect.

When we finally came up for air, laughing, my skin still buzzing, Shane threw me a grin and pulled the anchor.

"Time to head in," he said.

I stretched out, enjoying the last bits of sun, and the sound of the motor humming beneath us. We weaved through the canals, cutting through the water at a steady pace, my body still humming in post-bliss contentment.

Then, he slowed the boat and turned toward a neighborhood. I propped myself up on my elbows.

Where are we?

We drifted through a narrow waterway lined with massive houses, the kind with pristine docks and boats that cost more than my entire future.

I sat up fully. "Uh, Shane? Where are we going?"

He casually adjusted the throttle, looking way too at ease for my liking. "My dad's house."

I blinked, trying to process.

"No. Nope. Absolutely not." I scrambled for my cover-up, feeling very exposed in my tiny bikini.

Shane laughed. "What's the problem?"

I gaped at him. "THE PROBLEM? I can't meet your father while looking like I just walked off a Girls Gone Wild special, and I definitely can't meet him after what just happened on this boat."

He gave me a look like I was being dramatic. I wasn't being dramatic. I was traumatized.

And now, Shane was steering me directly into an impromptu meeting with his father.

Fan-fucking-tastic.

He gave me a sideways glance, clearly distracted. "I told my dad we'd stop by for a drink."

A drink with his father. After I'd just let Shane have his way with me on a boat in the middle of the goddamn Intracoastal.

I froze.

His dad's house, not his mom. Not another polite but distant introduction over salad. His father.

My pulse ticked up a notch. I thought meeting his mom was going to be a challenge. I didn't have the best track record of meeting mothers.

And dads usually love me. But with Shane's dad, it was a different kind of test. Shane lived for his father's approval. I had never seen him nervous before, never seen him try in front of anyone. But even before we got to the house, I could see it, the way he adjusted his hat, the way his fingers tapped anxiously against the wheel, the way his jaw locked like he was bracing himself.

I knew that look. Because I'd lived that look. I'd been that look. Waiting for someone's approval. Waiting to be enough.

And suddenly, I wasn't nervous for myself anymore. I was nervous for him.

Fuck it. We didn't have to do this. Let's turn around and head back to 15 minutes ago when my legs were draped around him. We could escape. No one would see us. We could make up some excuse about losing track of time.

We could...too late.

The back door to the house swung open and out stepped his dad. And his dad's wife, who, from what Shane had told me, started as the mistress.

Sweet Jesus, take the wheel.

They strolled down the dock, casual as anything, completely un-fazed, and before I could even attempt to throw myself into the water and swim away, they were handing us Captain and Cokes.

Like this was completely normal. Like this wasn't insane and I wasn't half-naked and internally spiraling.

I took the drink, mostly because I needed something to do with my hands. Shane took a long sip of his, clearly trying to calm his nerves. He finally smirked, bumping his shoulder against mine. I side-eyed him, sipping my drink, trying to pretend I wasn't dying inside. This was fine. This was totally fine.

At least, that's what I told myself. I watched him carefully, saw the way he leaned in just a little, waiting for his dad to say something. Anything.

A nod. A *"good to see you, son."* Some kind of acknowledgment.

It was subtle, but I saw it, and suddenly, I understood. Shane wasn't nervous because he was introducing me to his dad. He was nervous because he was still trying for his dad. Still waiting for that look of approval and hoping he was *enough*. And it made me want it for him. Made me want to be perfect for this man I had just met, even though I wasn't sure why I suddenly cared so much.

Because for the first time in my life, meeting someone's family wasn't excruciating. And Shane's family, they were easy, like him, and uncomplicated or unbothered. They were easy to love.

And just like that, I felt myself falling even harder.

~ele~

The moment happened so fast. One minute, I was sipping my Captain and Coke, making polite small talk with Shane's father, pretending like I wasn't still slightly uncomfortable standing there in a bikini.

The next, the floor vanished beneath me. Because Shane's father, casual as ever, leaned back in his chair, swirled the ice in his drink, and asked, "So, how was California?"

My stomach twisted. I set my drink down slowly, too slowly. Like my body was buying time for my brain to catch up.

Shane went to California? That was news to me. Sure, I had picked him up from the airport last week. He told me what time to be there, and I—like an absolute idiot—showed up, no questions asked. Because I trusted him and thought if I needed to know anything, he'd tell me.

But now, I had questions. And one very specific answer was already forming in my mind. California. His ex lived in California.

I glanced at Shane. His jaw tensed for a second. Just long enough to confirm what I already knew. The weight of it settled over me like lead. I should have seen it. Should have known. It was in the way he hesitated, the way his fingers tightened just slightly on the beer bottle, the way his father had unknowingly unraveled his perfectly spun lie in just a few casual words.

And I was just standing there, watching the final thread snap. I exhaled slowly, tapping my fingers against the armrest, watching him.

"Shane?" I said, keeping my voice light. Neutral.

He turned toward me, smiling like this was no big deal. "Yeah?"

"You never mentioned your trip was to California."

He shrugged. "Didn't think it was important."

I nodded slowly. "Right. Not important."

Silence stretched. A long, suffocating silence.

His father, oblivious, retreated to the kitchen to get the steaks ready for grilling. Shane reached for his beer, eyes flicking away. I let the moment linger, let the weight of his words sit between us.

I tilted my head. "You went to California to, what? Tie up some loose ends?"

His beer hovered at his lips. He didn't respond. Because we both knew the answer.

Shane sighed. "Sam."

I held up a hand. "No."

And suddenly, it all clicked. The realization hit like a wrecking ball. If he flew halfway across the country—across the damn continent—to see her, then he sure as hell wasn't over her. A man doesn't make that level of effort unless he's still pining.

Which meant that on the night of his birthday? When I knocked on his door? When I stood there, waiting, wondering where he was? He was with her.

Lost his phone? Slept at Barrett's?

I was a fucking idiot. I swallowed hard, my pulse hammering in my ears. We might not have been exclusive at the time of the offense, but he lied. He had looked me square in the face and lied. Like a goddamn sociopath. Just fucking lied.

And the worst part was how effortless it was for him. The way it fell from his lips, smooth and practiced, like he was reciting the weather. Like lying to me, deceiving me, was second nature. And that, was unforgivable.

Like so many others before him, he had play me like a fool.

I bit the inside of my cheek, turning back to his father walking through the back door, with my best attempt at an effortless smile. "Excuse me, I need a refill," I said, standing up and grabbing my empty glass.

I needed a moment. A second to process the undeniable rage building in my chest. I didn't want to make a scene so I didn't ask more questions. Because, let's be real, I already knew the answers.

Shane didn't try to stop me. He just watched me walk away.

And that silence. That told me everything I needed to know.

—— ✐ℓℓ ——

The boat ride back to his friend's place was quiet. I sat there, staring at the water, the salty wind tangling my hair, pretending like my stomach wasn't a knot of betrayal.

Shane tried. He made a few comments, joking about the cookery of the steaks. I responded in clipped sentences.

Because what was I supposed to say?

"Hey, Shane, funny story, I just found out you cheated and lied, and I'd really love to deep-dive into that over the sound of gently lapping waves and a fucking sunset."

Instead, I just let the silence stretch. Let it fester. Shane exhaled, clearly feeling the shift, but not quite sure what to do with it.

The boat cut through the water, taking us back to shore. And I counted down the minutes until we were off it. Because I wasn't about to do this here. Not in the middle of the ocean.

Not where I couldn't get away.

We sat on the bed in the guest room. I had just gotten out of the shower, scrubbing the salt air and chaos off my skin, trying to cleanse myself of the whole damn day. Shane stood across from me, unpacking his toiletries. Moving through the motions, about to hop in the shower like nothing was wrong. Like he hadn't just spent an entire boat ride home in tense, suffocating silence. And I hadn't just figured out *everything*.

I clenched my jaw, eyes locked on the TV, barely registering the silent show playing on mute. *Friends* on syndication. Go figure.

In that moment, I was reminded of Craig—the boyfriend who treated me like a queen and worshipped the ground I walked on. And how did I reciprocate those feelings? With bare minimum effort and the same thoughtless behavior. I cheated. Perhaps my action was a more egregious, though, because Shane and I weren't together that long before his indiscretion. I, on the other hand, had been with Craig for years. I'd spent years with a man who loved me, and that was how I decided to treat him? Sadly, I never loved him the way he loved me, but he deserved far more than what I gave him. Now, look how the tides had turned.

Before I could stop myself, I asked, "When were you going to tell me?"

Shane froze, toothbrush in hand.

"Tell you what?"

I turned to him slowly.

"That you went to California to see her."

Silence.

Then, "I didn't—"

"Shane."

He exhaled sharply, running a hand through his hair. "Sam, it wasn't—"

"The night of your birthday?" I interrupted, my voice like ice.

His eyes flicked to mine, just for a second. And that did it. That was all I needed to see.

I laughed. Because of course. I let that sit between us, the weight of it pressing the air from the room.

"So let me get this straight," I said, my voice shaking now, not weak, just furious. "You fucked her the night of your birthday. Lied about it. Came to my house the next morning like nothing happened. Slept in my bed. Then—THEN—you had the audacity to have me pick you up from the fucking airport like I was your personal Uber after you just spent an entire week with her?"

Shane stared straight ahead, silent. Resigned. He wasn't defending himself or apologizing. He wasn't even trying to deny it anymore. He just sat there, like a man who had nothing left to say. He could see it on my face, the finality.

I inhaled slowly through my nose, pressing my lips together, holding back the burn of humiliation.

Finally, he shifted. Desperate for a change in scenery, for an escape, he said, "I'm going to take a shower. Then we'll talk about this, and I'll tell you everything."

I just stared at him.

He turned, walked into the bathroom. and shut the door. The shower turned on. And I moved. Quietly and methodically. I grabbed my bag, zipped it shut, and slipped out the door. The

Uber I had ordered ten minutes ago was already waiting in the driveway.

"Take me to the airport," I told the driver.

The car pulled away. I sat there, staring out the window. No music, and no calls. Just the roar of my own fury.

I was done. Actually done this time.

Because I didn't just feel betrayed. I felt trapped.

The walls were caving in, closing in so fast that I could barely breathe.

And I knew if I stayed, if I let him talk his way out of it, if I let myself believe him, I would lose. So I booked the next flight home. And I left.

Because Shane was exactly who I thought he was.

And I knew this game was over.

The Proposal

"Boston – Augustana"

I can't believe it happened. I can't believe I didn't see it coming. I can't believe I said yes.

Yes, to becoming this man's wife. Yes, to spending the rest of my life with him. And of all the men I highlighted in the aforementioned chapters—the liars, the charmers, the commitment-phobes, the ones who made me seriously contemplate arson—to think HE would be the one to finally seal the deal?

Wild. Perhaps I should start from the beginning. Because, let me tell you, there had definitely been a point where I had considered becoming a nun. Not even a half-hearted, "Maybe I'll take a break from dating" kind of consideration.

No, a fully committed, where's-the-nearest-convent, take-me-to-the-nunnery, Lord-prepare-me-for-a-life-of-solitude type of moment.

I had sworn off love. Sworn off men. And had sworn off the constant, exhausting, soul-crushing heartbreak that both seemed to cause me.

And yet, here I was.

After what felt like a lifetime of cat and mouse, push and pull, dramatic exits, stubborn reunions, and me drafting at least three break-up texts I never actually sent—we finally got our shit together.

We stopped playing the games and we chose each other. It wasn't perfect. But it was ours. It was our love story.

What I've discovered about love is that no love story is perfect. And if anyone tries to tell you otherwise, they're either lying or delusional.

Think about it. You wander through this chaotic, unpredictable world, and out of the billions of people on this planet, you choose one. You choose to share your time, your space, and your life with them. That's terrifying. And special. But mostly terrifying.

I once received advice from a mentor when I was unhappy with my marketing job, feeling stuck and restless. Their words were so unexpectedly wise that I started applying them to everything—work, friendships, relationships.

"There will never be anything in life that makes you happy 100% of the time," they said. "It's just not realistic. You're a Type A overachiever, it's practically in your DNA to find flaws. But instead of focusing on everything that's wrong, ask yourself: How happy does this make me overall? Are you happy most days? 80% of the time? That's a win. But if you're miserable more days than not, if the good moments are just small flashes in an otherwise never-ending storm, then maybe it's time to move on."

That has always stuck with me. Because we live in an imperfect world, surrounded by imperfect people, yet we chase perfection like it's something we can actually catch. We hold love to impossible standards, expecting it to be effortless, painless, movie-script-level romantic. And when reality inevitably falls short, we convince ourselves it must not be real love.

But real love isn't flawless. It's messy and frustrating. It's learning how to sit with the hard moments instead of running from them. It's choosing someone, over and over again, even when it would be easier to walk away.

So I chose. I chose to take the leap. To lean into the fear instead of letting it push me away, and to trust in something that wasn't perfect, but was still right.

And that was absolutely worth it.

———

That's also how I found myself living with him.

"Playing house" was weirdly easy. Domestic bliss didn't make me want to crawl out of my skin. We fell into a rhythm—grocery shopping, arguing over what to watch on Netflix, taking turns stealing the good pillow at night.

Then came the holidays. Somewhere warm, my family decided. Somewhere sunny, where palm trees provide the best kind of shade, and coconut shells provide the best kind of drinks. A much-needed escape from the cold.

We packed our bags, checked our passports, and set alarms to ensure we were on time for the flight. And yet, because we are who we are, and couldn't keep our hands off of each other, we were frantically running out the door at the last possible second. Because honestly, does a quickie ever actually take 30 seconds?

Nah.

I was in my usual pre-trip panic mode, scanning every corner of our home with laser focus, making sure we weren't forgetting anything important—passports, chargers, underwear, dignity.

And that's when I saw it, sitting there on top of the dresser. Not hidden or tucked away in some "you'll-never-find-this" secret compartment. No. Just sitting there like a high school girl who's dying to spill all your secrets.

A little black box.

Now, I don't consider myself a naturally nosy person. *Okay. That's a lie.* But in this moment? I wasn't trying to snoop. I simply existed in the same space as the box, and it was practically screaming at me. At first, I didn't know what to make of it. Surely, it wasn't *that* kind of box. Surely, he wouldn't be *that* careless, leaving something that monumental out in the open like a takeout menu.

But curiosity is a bitch. So I picked it up, held it in my hands, and then, because I clearly have no self-control, I opened it.

And there it was. A diamond ring. A very real, very engagement-y ring.

Now, I don't want to jump to conclusions, but...WHAT ELSE COULD IT BE FOR?

A reward for good behavior? A fancy paperweight? A prank?

No. It was exactly what it looked like. An engagement ring. And suddenly, I forgot how to breathe.

My stomach flipped, my brain short-circuited, and my hands? Oh, they immediately snapped that box shut and placed it exactly where I found it as if I'd just activated an ancient curse and needed to undo the damage before the spirits came for me.

I took three steps back, hands in the air, as if the box could somehow sense my intrusion and would self-destruct at any moment. And then I ran. Not literally. But I exited the room like it was suddenly haunted. By the time I made it downstairs, he was checking his bag, casual as ever.

"Did we forget anything?" he asked.

I blinked. Thought about the very expensive, life-altering jewelry box I just violated. Shook my head.

"Nope! Looks good!" I said, voice an octave higher than normal.

He gave me a look as if he could sense I was acting weird.

"You sure?"

"Positive."

Then, like the pathological liar I had suddenly become, I added, "But, you know, you should double-check. Just in case."

And with that, I casually strolled to the car, sat in the passenger seat, and waited. And when he returned? His bag seemed... fuller. Maybe it was my imagination. Or maybe, he had shoved a tiny black box deep into the depths of his carry-on like his life depended on it.

I sat there, staring out the window, heart pounding, brain racing, realizing what this meant. He was going to propose.

HOLY SHIT.

And then, like a woman with no sense of self-restraint, I made the biggest mistake of all. At the airport, right before we boarded, he went to the bathroom and left me with his bag. You know, the one with the ring. It was just sitting there, taunting me.

And I told myself, Sam, DON'T. Don't ruin it. Don't look. Don't be that person.

But then, one little peek wouldn't hurt. So, naturally, I unzipped the bag, reached into the first pocket, and BOOM. There it was. Black box. First pocket I checked, like it was meant to be found.

And this time, I took my time. Opened the box and examined the ring. Let the reality truly sink in, because now, it was real. He wasn't just thinking about proposing. He wasn't just casually holding onto a ring for some future, distant, maybe-one-day moment.

It was happening and it was happening soon.

For the first time, I didn't panic. I just stared at it. At this tiny, perfect, life-changing piece of jewelry.

And whispered to myself, "Holy shit."

Our accommodations were something out of a dream, a villa ripped straight from the glossy pages of Travel & Leisure. It was spectacular. You step out of the first-floor living area, and your feet instantly met soft, sun-warmed sand. Just a few yards beyond, the ocean stretched endlessly, waves lapping gently at the shore as if they, too, were in no rush to leave.

It was secluded, serene, the kind of place where time slowed down and the rest of the world ceased to exist. Our villa was perched on what could only be described as a private island.

Well, private-ish.

By *our*, I mean me, my fiancé-to-be, my parents, my sister, her husband, their kids, and my aunts and uncles. You know, just the entire extended family. Nothing says romantic getaway quite like your mother asking if you've reapplied sunscreen for the third time that day.

But even with the chaos of family togetherness, the trip was incredible. We lounged by the pool, the water shimmering under the kind of tropical sun that made everything feel golden. We did water sports that tested the limits of our survival instincts, indulged in world-class cuisine, and drank cocktails out of coconuts like we were starring in our own resort commercial.

And yet, none of it held my attention. Because all I could think about was that damn ring. I was obsessed. Consumed by that little black box. It haunted me. It was like The Tell-Tale Heart, except instead of a dead man under the floorboards, it was a diamond ring lurking in my boyfriend's luggage.

When? When was he going to propose? Would it be at dinner? On a sunset stroll? Would I be mid-bite into a piece of sushi when he suddenly slid the ring across the table? Would I choke? Would that be how I died?

The suspense was killing me. And then, he started trying. He suggested a leisurely stroll on the beach. I declined. Not because I didn't want to be engaged, but because I refused to make it that easy on him. I knew what he was up to.

"Hey, wanna go walk on the beach so I can propose in front of children pummeling sand at each other, or an old man sunning himself in nothing but a Speedo?"

Absolutely not.

Then he tried again. A catamaran ride this time.

"Hey, wanna go on a sailboat so I can get down on one knee, but then immediately vomit all over you because I'm nervous and the boat is rocking just a little too much?"

Hard pass.

Every time he set up the perfect moment, I shut it down.

Because after everything we had been through, if this man truly wanted to marry me, he was going to have to work for it.

—ee—

We were nearing the final days of the trip. And it still hadn't happened yet.

Mind you, I was making it rather difficult on him, but we only had two days left before we headed back to reality. Back to cold weather, morning commutes, and grocery store runs that didn't include fresh mangoes from a beachfront stand.

If it was going to happen, it had to be soon. And I was pretty sure tomorrow was the day. He'd planned an excursion just for the two of us—hiking, petting monkeys, zip-lining our cares away. The kind of itinerary that screamed *he's going to propose*!

I stared at the ceiling, mentally running through all the ways it could happen. Would I be covered in sweat? Would my hair be matted to my face, looking like I'd just run a marathon? What if a monkey jumped on me mid-proposal and stole the ring?

I rolled out of bed thinking of all of the ways the engagement could go spectacularly wrong. Shaking off my overactive imagination, I stretched as I headed toward the bathroom. We still had about 30 minutes before we met the family for breakfast anyway.

He was still sleeping, peaceful, blissfully unaware of my internal spiral.

God, I love him.

Crazy how we got here. How we survived heartbreak and put our egos aside. How we found our way back to each other, despite all the reasons we shouldn't have. We were going to grow old together. We were going to keep making memories. Someday, there would be tiny little versions of us running around, filling our house with chaos and laughter. Right now, it was just us and our dog, Harper. But I imagined Harper watching over our kids with the same gentle patience she had when I tried to wrestle a sock from her jaws.

I smiled at the thought as I stepped toward the window, letting the bright morning light warm my skin. I ran my fingers through my hair, yawning as I stretched my arms overhead. The day was absolutely perfect. Crystal-clear water stretching to the horizon. The sun painted the sky in golden hues. The kind of day that felt like a promise. Maybe we'd get one last perfect swim in before packing up.

Then something caught my eye. A splash of red against the sand. I squinted. Was that... blood?

Immediate panic. Shark attack? Did someone lose a limb?

I leaned closer, my heart pounding, before reality smacked me in the face. Rose petals? A trail of rose petals. Leading to words etched into the sand.

Will You Marry Me?

I froze. Time stopped. My stomach plummeted. I blinked, trying to process whether I was dreaming or having an out-of-body experience. And then, he was there. Right next to me on one knee. Ring in his hands and tears in his eyes.

I turned to him, completely stunned. This wasn't how I thought it would happen. I had spent days obsessing over the proposal, replaying possible scenarios in my head like a rom-com montage. Would it happen on the boat? At dinner? During the zip-lining fiasco when I was strapped into a harness, trying not to scream?

And never did one of those scenarios play out like this. And it was absolutely, 100% perfect. I barely registered his words at first, my brain still buffering like a bad Wi-Fi signal.

Then his voice pulled me back in.

"Sam," he started, his voice thick with emotion, "I knew, before I even admitted it to myself, that you were it for me. You challenge me, make me laugh, drive me insane in the best possible way, and make every single day better just by being in it. There was never a doubt in my mind. It's always been you. It will always be you. Marry me?"

And all I could do was laugh. Not because I wasn't taking it seriously. Not because I was nervous or overwhelmed. But because he had actually pulled it off.

After all the overthinking, all the guessing, all the anticipation, he had still managed to completely, utterly surprise me.

I laughed because he knew. He knew I had seen the ring on the dresser. He knew I would overanalyze every single thing he did. And because of that, he had thrown me off the scent so spectacularly, so hilariously well, that I couldn't do anything but laugh at my obliviousness.

The beach walks? The boat ride? The planned excursion tomorrow? All of it was a goddamn decoy. While all along he had every intention of surprising me to ensure this moment was as magical as it could be.

I looked down at him, my heart swelling, my entire body buzzing.

And then, finally—

"Yes."

Because of course, it was always going to be yes. And as I felt his arms wrap around me, I realized I wasn't just choosing him in this moment. I was choosing every future moment.

Every lazy Sunday morning. Every inside joke. Every chaotic family gathering.

Every version of us that would come to be.

—ele—

So, who was the smug bastard who stole my heart?

Well, that's a chapter for another day...

Before you go...

Frolick is a series.

Not a cliffhanger-for-fun situationship.
Not an accidental open ending that makes you want to throw the book in a fit of rage.
It's a planned, intentional, fully thought-out series.

Frolick is the first book in a multi-book story. Sam's version comes first—but it's not the whole truth.

Don't fret, babes. Feel them feels. Just know this ending is exactly where it's supposed to be.

The Frolick Series

Book One: *Frolick*
Sam's version of events.
The meet-cutes. The red flags. The choices made with confidence and poor judgment.

Book Two: *Frolick: The Male Perspective*
The same story—from his side.
The parts you didn't hear. The thoughts he never said out loud.
The moments that look very different when you're inside his head.

Book Three: *Frolick: The Wedding*
The proof that sometimes the mess actually leads somewhere. The happily-ever-after (with complications).

Bonus Chapter

MALE POV: LEE

D inner at the firehouse was always the same: loud, messy, plates stacked higher than anyone felt like scrubbing. I drew dish duty that night, standing at the sink with suds up to my elbows, half-listening to the guys argue about who was the best cook. My body was running on autopilot. Twenty-four-hour shifts had a way of grinding you down until every chore blurred into the next.

The tones dropped mid-scrub. That familiar shriek over the PA, the one that never failed to cut straight through bone.

Another vehicle accident.

I let the dish clatter back into the sink and headed to grab my gear. We hadn't had a fire call in weeks, just a string of endless car wrecks.

Instantly, the boots slammed against concrete, the engine roared to life, and the doors rattled as they rolled open to the night. We loaded up, sirens blaring, and I did the usual mental prep. You get used to the chaos after a while—metal twisted, glass shattered, noise muffled under the weight of adrenaline. You learn how to shove the images down deep so you can do the job.

But when we pulled up, something in my gut clenched.

Headlights cut across the scene, landing on a single black car mangled against the guardrail, its frame folded in like a crumpled soda can. My gut twisted. The victim was still inside, and I could see long blonde hair covering the face of a young woman, about Sam's build.

And for a split second, I thought it was her.

Everything in me froze. My vision tunneled, blood roaring in my ears, and the only word in my head was her name.

Sam.

I was out of the truck before it fully stopped, feet pounding against pavement, my gloves half-pulled on as I ran toward the wreck. I was moving fast, too fast, my chest tightening with every step. My crew shouted, tried to direct traffic, but all I saw was the wreckage. The car crumpled. The body slumped forward.

Training told me to assess, to move steadily, to let my crew work the scene, but instinct shoved all of that aside. I had to see her face. I had to make sure it wasn't her.

Up close, the details sharpened. Same blonde hair, but not Sam's. Same frame, same size, same everything that had gutted me from a distance, but not her. Relief slammed into me so hard my knees nearly buckled.

But relief didn't last.

Because even if it wasn't her, it was somebody's Sam. Someone's granddaughter, daughter, or girlfriend. Someone's everything. And when we finally pried the door open, when we pulled her free and realized she hadn't made it, the weight of it hit me like a freight train.

My hands shook the entire time I worked. Steady on the outside, chaos underneath. I barked orders, cleared glass, kept my voice sharp, but inside I was falling apart. Because all I could see was what would've happened if it had been her. All I could feel was the knife-edge of how close I'd come to losing her without warning.

Lee didn't know if yet, but that night would change everything...

Acknowledgments Page

Well, well, well... would you look at that? I actually finished this thing. Who knew?

First and foremost, a massive thank you to my family, who, despite knowing all my flaws, still claim me in public. You've been my greatest adventure, my safe space, and the reason I know unconditional love exists.

To my sister – thank you for putting up with my obsessive overthinking, my random rants about character arcs, and for pretending to be just as excited about this book as I am. You're the real MVP, bird.

To Amber, Nicole, and Paura – thank you for pushing me to make this book the best version of itself. Your feedback and encouragement were the wind beneath my writing wings.

To my husband – none of this would have been possible without you. You believed in me and encouraged every idea (even the ones that made you uncomfortable), and gave me the space and support to chase something that mattered to me. Thank you for loving me through the chaos, for cheering the loudest, and for being my ride or die in every storm. I love you endlessly.

To my son – you are the reason I wake up each day determined to do more, be better, and chase big, wild dreams. Everything I do—this book, this journey, this life—is for you. I hope one day you read these words (maybe not the actual book, though) and know how much I adore you, how deeply I believe in you, and how proud I am to be your mom. I love you, Boo Boo Butt, times infinity.

To my parents – thank you, thank you, thank you for showing me the kind of person I strive to be. For giving me a safe space that I'll always carry with me and one I hope to recreate for my own family. You are my foundation, my compass, my constant inspiration. I love you more than words can express.

And to my readers – oh, you beautiful, incredible humans. If you've ever laughed, cried, or screamed at a text message after reading something in this book, then I consider my job here done. This one's for you.

And finally, a special shoutout to **love itself** – for being messy, unpredictable, beautiful, and absolutely worth the chaos.

Now, go forth and frolic(k). And maybe don't text your ex. (Or do. No judgment here.)

Stay in the Frolick Universe

If you're still thinking about these characters (you are),
still processing the ending (fair),
or already curious about what happens next (as you should)...

Scan the code below.

If you loved the mess, wait until you hear his side.

www.ingramcontent.com/pod-product-compliance
Lightning Source LLC
Chambersburg PA
CBHW020357110726
47899CB00006B/1751